ECHOES & ILLUSIONS

THE HUNTERS - BOOK 1

RORI BLEU

ROSIE CHAPEL

Echoes & Illusions

The Hunters - Book 1

A Dystopian Romance

by
Rori Bleu & Rosie Chapel

First printing: 2022
ISBN: 978-0-6451985-6-0 (ebook)
ISBN: 978-0-6451985-7-7 (paperback)

Ulfire Pty. Ltd.
P.O. Box 1481
South Perth
WA 6951
Australia

Cover Design: Rebecca Norman
Images Courtesy: Deposit Photos (Artists: Krivis and yekophotostudio).
Designed in Canva.

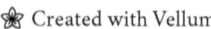 Created with Vellum

ACKNOWLEDGMENTS

RORI BLEU

Special thanks to...

Jean Forrester for helping bring the characters to life, as well as the story.

Terry Fielding for allowing me to spam her mailbox with rough drafts.

Annette Begeschke, Jo Anne Vesledahl, and **Sheri Meece** for being forced to continue beta reading.

Rebecca Norman for her extraordinary talent in developing the beautiful cover as well as her insistence in observing the rules of proper English.

ACKNOWLEDGMENTS
ROSIE CHAPEL

Thank you, Rori for your generosity in inviting me to be co-author in this amazing story, which I fell in love with when it was a third of its current length. Seriously… we should not be allowed to collaborate!
I am truly honoured.

Melanie Duval — for being badgered into reading the almost final draft — thank you. Your time and quick eye is much appreciated.

Thank you to my hubby for working his technical wizardry to publish the book… he's definitely a keeper!

AUTHORS' NOTE

A shortened version of this novella was originally published in 2019 (and *not* inspired by the current pandemic) in *With Love from Venice*, a Voyages of the Heart Anthology, under the title *For Love*.

Since then it has been revised extensively and lengthened substantially, transforming it into the story you are about to read. If fact happens to follow fiction, we'll plead the fifth!

Rori and Rosie

PROLOGUE

Mother Nature can be a vindictive bitch when men attempt to play God. Of all the weapons at her disposal, to punish them for their impertinence, she chose two of the most mundane to execute her bidding: a leaky valve and a summer breeze.

This scathing act occurred on a salt flat in the Nevada desert known as Groom Lake or, and more popularly, to the locals and the millions of conspiracy theorists around the world — *Area 51.*

In this desolate place, under the shroud of governmental secrecy, American scientists, busy experimenting with genetic material, inadvertently contaminated a water cistern.

Before the internet went permanently dark, chatrooms exploded, speculating that the material in question was alien in nature. That a probe sent to Mars to retrieve samples, had returned with more than just soil. A claim of which no one ever provided definitive proof and, the end, its origin was irrelevant.

What *was* relevant that bright, blustery day was a spigot inexplicably sprung a leak, allowing thousands of gallons of water to gush out over the arid wasteland. The toxic mixture evaporated under the glare of the desert sun, leaving the particles suspended in the air.

Mother Nature smiled. *Talk about the perfect opportunity.*

The gusty wind played into her hands, carrying the vapour eastward across the United States. Reminiscent of a swarm of locusts, it fanned out, cutting a swathe of annihilation in its path.

Neither did she limit her wrath to America, exploiting the jet stream which blew the deadly cargo across the Atlantic to Europe and points beyond.

Man, as a species, needed to pay the ultimate price.

By the time the winds had circumvented the Earth, half the planet's population had succumbed. No one was untouched, and those *lucky* enough to recover continued to endure the repercussions.

Too numerous to be disposed of, corpses accumulated as fast as leaves in autumn, spilling into the rivers and streams, choking off and contaminating sources of fresh drinking water.

The insidious blossoming of typhoid and cholera, precipitated a second wave of death. An atmosphere of terror pervaded every corner of the globe.

International pharmaceutical companies vied to develop countermeasures, experimenting with exotic cocktails of antivirals and antibiotics.

Normal rules did not apply.

Time was of the essence and, without the luxury of being

able to run the usual protracted battery of tests, the industry relied on government propaganda to persuade the survivors these miracle medicines would be their salvation.

Regrettably, the cure turned out to be more lethal than the disease and, too late, they realised Mother Nature cannot be halted by man's frenzied interference.

She simply mutated her weapon.

Adding insult to injury, the hapless victims who had placed their faith in the hands of their governments, discovered the virus, combined with the unproven antidotes, altered their DNA. So drastic was the corruption that, instead of it taking generations to evolve, the impact was immediate.

Like a cosmic crapshoot, no one could predict how they would change.

Some developed an increase in muscle mass, while an expanded mental capability affected others. It was hailed as a new beginning for humanity.

The jubilation was short-lived.

In a pattern repeated since the dawn of time, when differences elicit fear, civilisation reverted to type. As the genetic anomalies manifested, instead of embracing them, the remnants of humankind splintered off into societal groups.

The strong became farmers and learnt to cultivate the land by hand, as had their ancestors. By tacit consensus and, in a bid to derive a sense of preservation, they established enclaves in what remained of the cities around the world.

For those afflicted with an increased mental acuity, the gift... *or curse...* drove many insane. The ability to know everything, yet be unable to act on that knowledge, robbed them of empathy.

They became known as the Hunters.

Shunned by their so-called *civilised* counterparts, they too banded together but, chafing against the constraints imposed by society, chose a nomadic life. Viewing the existence of the cities' inhabitants as unnecessary, they grew to despise them, becoming little more than outcasts and psychotic predators, living for the thrill of the kill.

The ramifications of this *interference* stalked the succeeding generation.

Babies who were not stillborn, caused the deaths of their mothers. The dread of childbirth resulted in a significant decrease of pregnancies.

Technology, revered like the Gods of old, became another casualty. The knowledge and skill required to extract the necessary resources, to produce the innumerable so-called time saving devices and taken-for granted amenities, were lost in the aftermath.

Checkmate!

Mankind's demise seemed a certainty... or had Mother Nature at last found two souls deserving of her forgiveness?

1

Rome
New Era + 20 years
Autumn

Not even the mighty metropolis of Rome — historically, the religious epicentre for 1.3 billion believers of a past faith and former residence of God's emissary on Earth — was spared the horrific cataclysm which consumed the world.

An ancient city, born from the blood of Remus, spilled at the hands of his brother Romulus. The heart of a civilisation for millennia. An indomitable empire, forged by death and destruction, found itself burdened by a population where the dead overwhelmed the living.

Many fled the ravished, and now ironically dubbed, Eternal City.

Rome teetered on the precipice of abandonment, fated to be swept onto the ash heap of history.

Its salvation lay in the crafty hands of those who had seized control of the city at its fall.

Citizens who opted to remain within Rome were coerced by the ruling Council to construct a twelve-meter high, brick and cinder wall, which encircled the city in place of what used to be the teeming *Grande Raccordo Anulare* motorway.

The necessary materials for the project were plundered from the demolition of countless deserted buildings located too close to the proposed path of the towering fortification.

Aware the strenuous labour required reimbursement; the authoritarian regime came up with a plan to keep as many skilled people as possible within the walls. They awarded land, and living space, in lieu of payment. A grateful work-force was a loyal workforce.

To be fair, most agreed the soaring ramparts, complete with assorted gates — installed to control the flow of indi-viduals in and out of Rome — offered ample protection. A conviction the self-styled ruling aristocracy capitalised on with regularity.

That did *not* preclude these same elitists from seques-tering themselves, their families, and their brigades of mercenary guards behind the additional security of the imposing walls of the Vatican City — once a sovereign state.

These extra measures allowed the city's leaders to spend less time worrying about their precarious safety, and deluded the public into believing they were culturally superior to the few other surviving pockets of population. A delusion enhanced by the vast collection of untouched art and archi-tecture within its walls... even if barely a handful recognised their significance.

The average citizen deemed them superfluous. They had neither the time nor the desire to view any of it. Their ener-gies were focused on eking out a living not taking a class in art appreciation.

Overall, their existence was fragile, at best.

Gabriel awoke with the sun. Gingerly, he eased from the bed so as not to wake Bianca. She had been up most of the night, suffering bouts of nausea from the pregnancy.

Privately, the doctor had expressed his concerns to Gabriel about Bianca's condition this late into the third trimester, but neither of the expectant parents would agree to a termination.

Dressing for another day of harvest, he smoothed his jet-black hair with his hands. The mirror reflected the image of a man whose tanned skin testified to a life working in the oft harsh outdoors, while his soft brown eyes spoke of a kindness, rare these days.

A subtle change in light drew his eyes to their open bedroom window. Pink and purple hues, tinged with gold, bled over the distant peaks, infusing life into the earth — a transformation he felt privileged to witness.

With no time to linger, he took one last peek at his slumbering woman, her hair tousled about her pillow in a sooty mass, framing her face, and smiled at her gentle snores. Her ferocious denial of doing so, always made him laugh.

He had found the raven-haired beauty with the piercing ebony eyes wandering aimlessly in his fields during a blizzard the previous season. Her tattered clothes, negligible protection against the ferocious storm.

That *anyone* imagined he would turn her away was beyond him.

Besides, she was a true blessing, throwing herself into the backbreaking manual labour undertaken by all those working in the fields. Standing alongside him as they tended the vines while struggling with the pregnancy.

The baby.

Gabriel's gaze slid to the rise concealed by the blankets.

He felt a twinge of shame for not quashing the naysayers when they questioned his paternity, just because Bianca fell pregnant with what some considered unseemly haste.

The doctor did not query it, and Gabriel, who knew the child was his — unequivocally, assumed everyone else would react with similar disinterest.

They didn't but, instead of setting them straight, he chose to ignore the rumours and, in the early months, Bianca had borne the brunt of mean-spirited gossips. She paid no heed, saying they were jealous — the men because Gabriel had her, and the women because Bianca had won Gabriel.

In the same vein, he never felt the need to press her for details of her life before they met. People rarely discussed their pasts; everyone had a story of pain and loss.

It was better to live for the day and forget everything else. The future was not assured.

Leaning down, he brushed a kiss to her head and whispered a reminder the doctor would call by later to check on her. He chuckled when she mumbled an unintelligible acknowledgment and rolled away from him.

He would do anything for this woman.

He descended the polished wooden staircase to the ground floor. Previously, the narrow building they inhabited had served as apartments for as many as thirty occupants. Now, thanks to the backbreaking efforts of his younger days on the wall, the entire premises belonged to the couple.

It had cost Gabriel fifty percent of the next two seasons' harvests, to repurpose each of the four floors, but he spared no expense when it came to Bianca.

He had transformed the topmost level into sleeping quarters, which included a spacious bathroom.

A welcoming great room occupied the entirety of the

third floor, complete with ornamental fireplace. Perched below was the family's dining room and, on the ground floor, the kitchen with its eat-in nook.

Bianca had pleaded with Gabriel to settle closer to the centre of Rome, but he was not to be swayed. Located near the city's northwest gate and only a short hike to his fields — the erstwhile *Riserva Naturale della Marcigliana* — the house was perfect for him.

The four thousand hectares of the former reserve had been converted to farmland and divided up among those willing to cultivate it. Gabriel had bartered for multiple plots to raise both a vineyard and an apple orchard.

The commitment required was gruelling and many floundered. Their failure benefitted Gabriel who was able to purchase additional tracts of land at a fraction of their value. These, he rotated between wheat, and feed corn for the city's livestock.

Aware Bianca thought him addled for choosing to set out before the dawn chorus had begun to tune up, Gabriel preferred to start his day in the cool before the sunrise. After several years of trial and error, he had worked out the optimum time to harvest the fruit was early in the morning, while it was better to gather the other crops as the day warmed.

Gabriel dallied in the kitchen long enough to procure a loaf of bread and a jug of water, then hurried from the house.

Winding through the narrow streets to the gate, he nodded and flashed his identification to the guard as he left the confines of the city. Bearing in mind it was the same man on duty every morning, it seemed a ridiculous ritual.

But, rules were rules.

The morning sun had cleared the horizon by the time he reached his first stop. He paused to take in a breath of the fresh morning air, a daily habit which never failed to invigorate him. Proud of his hard-earned success as a farmer, Gabriel chalked it up to the sweet fragrance of his grapes.

Hooking the strap of his basket over his shoulder, he began to harvest the fruits of his labour. He selected the plumpest grapes discarding any undesirable specimens around the stems of vines to be used as fertiliser.

As the day progressed, it pleased Gabriel how quickly one basketful followed the next. He would have plenty of grapes to barter with the merchants in the market for whatever supplies Bianca and he might need to see them through the approaching winter.

The sun had reached its zenith before Gabriel registered that his neighbour's field remained unattended. Unease prickled at the back of his head. At the same moment, he heard the thud of footsteps in the fresh soil, and spun about, muscles taut, ready to defend himself.

His potential attacker turned out to be Bianca who tried to control her laughter as she wove her way through the vineyard, carrying a basket of food for their noon meal.

"Were you expecting the Diavolo?" she sassed.

"No, but I was not expecting Megaera, either." Gabriel smiled as he took her in his arms, hugging her as best he could, given her swollen belly. "Should you not be at home waiting for the doctor? He charges me for the trip whether you are there or not."

"Call that leech-herder a doctor all you want. To me he is just a greasy, old pervert who gets his jollies touching me in ways only you should. I swear to the gods I will strangle him with his stethoscope the next time he tries to *measure* my cervix!"

Shaking his head, chuckling, Gabriel tried to reason with

his woman. "I am sure all of Rome would be displeased if you killed their only doctor. Might I suggest a well-placed kick, instead?"

"I will consider it, my love, but enough talk of the bastard. Right now, I have come to feed you more than a prisoner's meal. You will need your strength not only to carry you through the rest of the day..." Bianca's fingers slipped down to the inseam of Gabriel's breeches, grazing playfully across the bulge swelling beneath her talented touch, "...but into tonight as well."

His chuckle became a growl "You truly are a Fury woman."

"As long as I am *your* Fury, my love I am happy. Though right now, you will eat and then we will finish the harvest."

Spreading a blanket on the ground, she set out sundry meats and cheeses for the pair. Her eyes kept wandering to their neighbour's property, noticing, as Gabriel had, that there was no one around.

"Are we missing a city holiday?" She nodded at the empty field.

Gabriel, shovelling a few pieces of sliced meat into his mouth, replied between chews, "I wish I had an answer for you. It's not like Garibaldi to be so late."

"Perhaps he is ill, or finally found his own woman to leer at, or partook a little too much of the fermented grapes you gave him for his lack of luck." Bianca grinned as she offered logical reasons why their friend was missing.

"When we are done here, maybe we ought to check on him," Gabriel suggested. "I would hate to think I was responsible for his grains going to seed. We would never get rid of him over the winter."

"Bah, your wines are so delicious, we never will anyway."

The pair shared a laugh, and the rest of the meal, before they resumed the arduous toil.

Bianca did her best to hide her discomfort, but Gabriel could sense it all the same and made sure to empty her basket quicker than usual.

Spending equal time tending to Bianca as he did the vines, meant the days' harvest took longer than normal, but Gabriel was thankful for the company. Not only did he love watching the beads of sweat cling to Bianca's beautifully plump body while she worked, but the absence of his neighbour had left him on edge.

The pair finished as the sun began to sink into the Tyrrhenian Sea. Gathering up the baskets, they made their way home.

2

————

In the distance, the couple could see the welcoming glow from the multitude of torches positioned strategically around the heart of the city. Determined to dissuade any of their unwanted neighbours from staging a surprise raid, the municipal leaders ensured every corner of the Piazza San Pietro was brightly lit. It was commonplace.

Not commonplace were the extra torches on the roofs of the old St. Peter's Basilica and the Papal Palace. The additions heralded trouble.

The shadows were lengthening, and Gabriel muttered to Bianca that they ought to hurry. It was one thing to be out past sundown within the relative safety of the walls, quite another to be exposed in the fields.

Every sound around them seemed to amplify, as if signalling some impending doom. Gabriel was positive the waning light of day concealed the source of their deaths because they had let time escape them.

Their reward for gaining their harvest became of secondary importance to preserving their lives.

Discovering their usual gate into the city unattended, did nothing to assuage their disquiet.

Bianca was the first to spot the bobbing lights coming in their direction. She shoved Gabriel into a convenient thicket of Cupressus. The needles and branches bit into their flesh as they tried to camouflage themselves.

In silence, they watched the marauders flee through the gate. Each had a bag slung over their shoulders, no doubt prizes from their audacious sortie into the outskirts of the city.

It was the female hurrying behind the rest who caught Bianca's eye. Her gasp of recognition snagged Gabriel's attention.

Signalling her to hush, they remained hidden in the bushes until the pursuing city guards had passed. After Gabriel checked to make sure the coast was clear, he guided her back onto the path.

He chided her in undertones. "Were you trying to get us killed? For the sake of the gods, you might as well have put out a banner and invited them in with us."

Bianca knew her exclamation had endangered them both. *How can I justify my actions without revealing I am no stranger to the invaders — especially my own sister?*

"Did you not see what the one at the end was carrying, you fool?" she parried. "That was the rug I wove Garibaldi for the planting festival!"

Grabbing Gabriel by the arm, she dragged him back to the main pathway. A tell-tale red trail marred the paving stones.

Gabriel did not need Bianca to explain what had happened, but she was going to anyway.

"I'll hazard that they stuffed the trophies from their hunt inside the rug. And knowing how large it is, I suspect they have been in the city for a while."

A frown creased Gabriel's face. He knew it was foolish to bother checking on their friend. Presumably they would find little more than a decapitated corpse.

The Hunters never took the bodies, they were too burdensome. Displaying the heads of their prey was enough to quench their bloodlust. It was a practice copied from their ancestors who paraded the heads of any animals they had slain.

To the Hunters, humans were the only prize worth mounting.

Reaching their house, Gabriel saw the front door had been kicked open and there was blood splattered over the frame.

Pulling his only *weapon* — a pair of pruning shears — from his belt, he begged Bianca to wait outside.

Slowly, he crept through the doorway and edged across the atrium. The lights of the city gave way to the gloom of the interior. Gabriel strained his eyes, willing them to catch the smallest of movements in the obscurity.

Hearing a sound behind him, he glanced over his shoulder to see the pregnant shape of Bianca picking her way towards him, in clear indication he had wasted his breath.

Stopping to argue the fact will prove just as ridiculous.

Following the hallway, which led to their kitchen, Gabriel stumbled over something. Instinctively, to avoid falling face-first, his hands shot out to prop himself against the walls.

Crouching, he felt what lay on the floor. "You do not need to worry about getting groped by the doctor anymore," he murmured.

Straightening up, he felt along the wall for one of the sconces. Retrieving the flint from his pocket, he lit the candles. One by one, they illuminated the remains of the city's recently departed physician... minus the man's head.

Bianca could not help herself. "I am betting the next one they find will not be making house calls."

It struck Gabriel as odd that Bianca neither screamed nor fainted at the sight of the headless doctor, and instead found it germane to crack a joke. *Perhaps this was not the first time she had seen a mutilated body.*

A conversation for later. Right now, they had other things to which they must attend.

"Hopefully, our visitors did not see fit to ransack the barn. We shall need the cart to transport the good doctor back to town."

Bianca muttered, "Why not let the currents of Tiber carry him back to the Castel and save us the trip."

"Beg pardon?" Gabriel asked as he stooped to pick up the body.

"I said, we should take some currants to save another trip."

Squeezing past Gabriel, Bianca entered the kitchen and busied herself packing jars of jams and preserves to convey to the market. Her soft humming reached Gabriel's ears.

Heaving the corpse onto his shoulder, he frowned and hesitated. *They had a dead man in their house, and she was humming?* He was about to remark upon her odd reaction, when the melody came to an abrupt halt.

"What are you waiting for? Permission to take the smelly old reprobate. Go," she flapped her hands in a shooing motion, "harness Ollie. If you insist on dragging me out after dark, the least you can do is treat me to a night in one of the better inns. We can sell our wares in the morning."

Astonished at her nonchalance, Gabriel swallowed the comment on the tip of his tongue. Shifting his balance, he headed for the small barn he had built in the courtyard beyond the house, casting Bianca a bewildered glance as he crossed the room.

After hurling the city's former physician into the back of the cart, he woke Ollie, their trusty grey donkey, from his slumber, who brayed his disapproval at being disturbed.

Bridle and harness fastened; Gabriel stroked the creature's forehead soothingly. "I sorry, Ollie, we have to go into town. You'll be happy to know, as a reward for your sacrifice, you'll be spending the night in stables usually reserved for the elite's ponies. Seems we will not be returning this eve."

3

Traffic on the narrow roads was heavier than usual, as though everyone in Rome had the same idea; to seek refuge within Vatican City.

Even though the incursion was limited to the outskirts of Rome, the fear was not. Inevitably, alarm spread like wildfire, stirring the populace into believing an all-out invasion was in progress, inciting a mad dash to where they felt safest.

The fortunate would be granted sanctuary within St. Peter's Basilica, while a select few would gain shelter in the more secure, and eminently more comfortable, Papal Palace.

If that was not troublesome enough, vendors sought to profit from the influx of people, adding to the congestion.

Caught up in the tide of humanity determined to demand the same protection as those who... supposedly... had the best interests of the city at heart, Bianca and Gabriel almost missed their intended crossing — the Ponte Sant'Angelo, which led to the Castel of the same name.

Thankfully, Gabriel's steady hands on the reins, and a donkey who responded quickly to his master's touch prevented a tricky detour. Gabriel spotted a gap, and Ollie swerved to the right, through the crush, to clip-clop safely across the bridge.

With its circular construction, formidable walls, and limited access points, Castel Sant'Angelo had been chosen by the triumvirate as their seat of power, as well as the civil offices which served the daily needs of the average citizen.

This location also meant the riffraff had no reason, except in cases of extreme emergencies, to enter the Vatican.

The same could not be said for the couple currently approaching the contingent of guards posted on the pathway. Emergency — no, extreme — arguably. They had no doubt, their cargo would accord them admittance not only into the Castel, but also right to the Council's chambers.

The sentries, weapons at the ready, caused Ollie to hesitate, earning him an encouraging tap on his hindquarters. Lurching forwards, the donkey nearly bowled over the Captain of the Nightwatch before the cart came to a complete stop.

Seeing the disdain on the captain's face, Gabriel begged forgiveness, "I am sorry, sir. The creature is a trifle jittery this evening."

"Is not all of Rome," the man huffed, giving the cart a cursory inspection.

With the end of his halberd, he lifted the edge of the tarp, shaking his head at the sight which met his eyes. He had lost track of the number of grisly remains which had passed him this evening, relieved somebody else had to dispose of the bodies.

"Take it over to the Courtyard of the Angel and dump it with the rest," he ordered. "The city is trying to identify the victims with due haste."

Bianca piped up, "We can save you the trouble. It's Dr Vincenzo."

"*What?*" The captain expostulated, not sure he had heard the woman correctly.

"It's the good doctor, I assure you," Bianca consoled, making sure not to let the exasperated sigh slip over her lips. "It appears, the poor man ran afoul of the pillagers ransacking our building."

The jaded soldier waved off the rest of her story.

Changing his instructions, he pointed to a line of rusting metal posts adjacent to the entrance. "Tie your donkey over there and take the body to the cells. Do not stop to talk to anybody on the way."

The sigh Bianca had been fighting to suppress broke free. "Why can we not just leave him with the rest? Have we not done our good deed for tonight by delivering him to you?"

"Are you *insane*, woman?" the captain snapped. "If the city is in uproar now, can you *imagine* what would happen if they learnt their only physician is among the victims?"

Gabriel patted Bianca on the knee in a placatory manner. Presumably, fatigue and stress of the pregnancy had loosened her tongue.

Bianca glared at the captain for a moment before tossing her hands up and relenting with a disgusted, "Fine. If we must."

"We will see your orders are carried out," Gabriel appeased the sentry, directing Ollie to the allocated spot.

Following behind, the sentry watched the pair alight from the cart, and the woman steer the donkey to one of the posts, muttering to the beast the entire way.

As if sensing the captain was eavesdropping on their private conversation, Bianca shot him another scowl.

She looped the donkey's reins around one of the metal rings which had been affixed to the old security barriers, expressing her displeasure at their treatment to the docile creature.

The need to remove himself from the sharp eyes of the woman, propelled the guard to the rear of the wagon. He was surprised to discover the man had already hefted the tarp-wrapped corpse onto his shoulder, inwardly perplexed as to why he loitered with what was obviously a heavy load.

The woman joined him, and the couple proceeded to the Castel's entrance.

Light dawned, making the captain appreciate being single. He shouted after them, "Once you have delivered your package, report to Chambers."

The ominous tone of this final command concerned Gabriel, but arguing would get them nowhere. He flexed his shoulders to distribute the weight of his burden more evenly, and fell into step behind Bianca.

The couple ascended the lengthy curves of the ramped corridor and trudged up two staircases before emerging into the Courtyard of the Angel on the third floor, where they saw the row of neatly arranged bodies, all in the same condition as Gabriel's burden. One end of each sheet was blood soaked, indicating where their heads had been.

Even though death for these poor souls had only come in the past few hours, a swarm of blowflies had assembled around the remains.

Gabriel bowed his head at the gruesome display, giving it a solemn frown, while Bianca appeared oblivious to the horror.

An arrow above a sign on the wall directed them across the Hall of Apollo, past the Hall of Justice — at which Bianca sniggered — and into the Courtyard of Alexander. Gabriel was just beginning to question whether the sentry had sent them on a wild goose chase, when they stumbled across the staircase leading to the cells on the floor below.

He heaved a sigh of relief; Dr Vincenzo had been a slight man in life, but the canvas encased corpse felt as if it was gaining weight with each step.

The couple paused at the pitch-black void waiting to swallow them whole if they dared descend the ancient stone steps.

Gabriel nudged Bianca and nodded at the sconces. "Grab one of the torches."

"Why can't we just toss him down?" Bianca asked, without looking at him. "The sentry was not specific about *where* we should leave the body."

"*Bianca...*" Gabriel was flabbergasted by her callous attitude.

Yanking the torch from its hold, she swept past him to lead the way down the stairs, effectively curtailing his censure.

Throughout the centuries, the cells of the Castel had served a variety of purposes. Not only a prison, they had been used to store grain and vast quantities of oil — the capacity of the latter being about 22,000 litres. While in the main, a food source, boiling oil was a very useful deterrent when poured on marauders.

For decades, the cool, dry atmosphere had provided the ideal environment for dedicated conservators who spent their days preserving priceless artefacts which, previously, graced this and many of the other museums and galleries scattered throughout the city. Since the catastrophe, the rooms had been reduced to storage vaults — such expertise regarded as unnecessary.

In truth, it was a lost skill.

Following the decision to convert Sant'Angelo into the Council's headquarters, the majority of artworks were either appropriated by the museum within Vatican City or commandeered by the elite to embellish their own apartments.

Nevertheless, when the couple entered the darkened chamber, the torch Bianca placed into a sconce by the door, illuminated several pieces by renowned artists and sculptors. Undergoing restoration, it was apparent they had been abandoned — in some cases, mid-brush stroke — on the day the plague befell the city, and here they remained, perched in their easels or on their plinths collecting dust.

Silent eyes on faces neither recognised, awaited the return of the talented few who had been in the process of reviving them.

Sadly, they never would.

As Gabriel lowered the doctor's body onto a wooden trestle table, he noticed Bianca turning a gold bowl in her hands. The muted metal shimmered dully in the flame of the torches.

"It's a shame," Bianca said, contempt thick in her voice. "Even with people dropping dead around them, men were still willing to sacrifice their lives for this poxy pisspot." She tossed it back, on the workbench where it landed with a clatter. "Greed," she muttered.

"Well, *amore mio*, do you suppose a mere two decades is long enough to override five thousand years of man's lust for wealth?"

Sometimes, Bianca was surprised by how insightful her man could be.

Closing the gap between them, she balanced on her tiptoes to brush a kiss to his lips. "No, and it makes me happy you remain a simple man with simple tastes and modest means."

Drawing her flush to his tall frame, he kissed her deeply, snarling his fingers through the knotted bun of her hair, as their passion intensified. Gabriel felt Bianca's nails dig into his chest, and his hands gravitated to her supple ass, preparing to hoist her onto the table.

With the recently deceased doctor missing his head, the only witnesses were the lifeless eyes on the canvases surrounding them, unable to turn away.

As his fingers tightened around the curve of Bianca's butt, she cried out and clutched her belly. Despite guessing she was going into labour, Gabriel asked stupidly, "Are you okay?"

Trying to catch her breath, she gasped between pants, "Your child does not approve of what you have planned."

He kissed her forehead lightly, "We will have plenty of time to practice for brothers and sisters."

A statement they both knew held no certainty.

"We best not leave the Council waiting." Bianca collected herself.

"True enough, my love. The sooner we get this over with, the sooner we can turn in for the night."

"Bah, you just want to get me into bed."

Gabriel shrugged his shoulders and grinned boyishly.

4

etracing their steps from the cells to the Courtyard of the Angel, they continued up to the fourth floor of the onetime Papal residence.

Today, it served as the Council's Chambers.

Gabriel and Bianca ascended the stairs, occasionally spying magnificently decorated rooms. They crossed the lavish *Sala Paolina* with its sumptuous stuccoes, and along the frescoed corridor to the Library. Although breathtaking, the extravagance screamed of man's fatuous attempts to express power in terms of gold and silver, which saddened the couple.

When they reached the large, mahogany doors, which functioned as the final line of protection for the trio who presided over the city, Bianca and Gabriel were stopped by the two guards.

"You are expected," the one on the right intoned. He knocked twice on the polished panelling, then opened the doors.

Momentarily, the three men ensconced in high-backed chairs behind a ridiculously ornate desk on a raised platform, were of secondary importance to the exquisite, vaulted ceiling, which captured the attention of the newcomers as they entered.

A not-so-subtle shove ushered them forwards.

Under the guise of establishing a *better* system of government, the Council had replaced democracy with an authoritarian administration. A right determined when their respective families claimed victory following the anarchy which engulfed the city when the last member of the former Italian government succumbed to the plague.

Control of the country's weaponry, as well as the right to rule, went to those with the strongest private armies.

The oldest member of the council, Cosimo Regillus — a man whose mother clearly had visions of grandeur when she chose his name — sat in the middle seat and was the only one of the trio to speak. "Explain the suffering you have caused our city."

Gabriel was confused that the tribunal dared accuse Bianca and himself of a crime before either of them had opened their mouths. "Surely, *Vostro Onore*, you have mistaken us for another scheduled to stand before your court. We come before you to report—"

"*Sì*, the death of the city's sole physician, Signore Vincenzo. Why were you not in your home to prevent this catastrophe?"

"With all due respect, *Vostro Onore*, no one in the city could have known this attack would occur," Gabriel argued, scrabbling to fathom the reason for Signore Regillus' preposterous, if veiled, allegation. "Not even the city guards were prepared for the Hunters."

"But if you knew you would not be home, why did you not send word to the city and save him the trip, not to mention his life." Anger rose in the councilman's voice. "We are helpless against even the most minor of illnesses now."

"It is not our fault," Gabriel objected. "My woman was home the entire morning and came to join me only when Dr Vincenzo failed to arrive at the appointed time. Is that not so, Bianca?"

The attention of the whole room swivelled to Bianca.

She had remained silent thus far but, with four pairs of eyes on her, it was no longer an option... neither did she care if it was.

"Look at you, three pompous asses sitting on your thrones, jumping to conclusions without investigating the facts. It is true, I left the villa this morning. There was work to be done and, since we never expect to receive offers of assistance from anyone within the walls of your lofty citadels, we must manage on our own."

Bianca paused to allow the weight of her condemnation of the city's hierarchy to sink in before adding, "Should I have waited for your lecherous old man? Given the course of events, I thank whatever gods you're praying to today, I did not."

"*Silenzio, donna.*" Infuriated, a pregnant woman had the audacity to speak to him with such disrespect, Signore Regillus leapt to his feet, his Italian heritage rearing its outraged head, scarlet and white mottling his pudgy face. "I recommend, farmer, you muzzle your woman before she puts your heads on a block."

Familiar with the steely resolve in Bianca's eyes, Gabriel knew walking across the Tiber would be easier than shutting her up. Nor was he naïve. The Council needed a scapegoat for the doctor's senseless death, and the two of them fit the bill.

Bianca's hormone fuelled agitation compelled her to continue her castigation. "How dare you try to pit my man against me? He has shown great restraint and respect for the lot of you. *Honours...?*" her lip curled scornfully. "...I had to bite my tongue to curb my laughter."

"I will not tell you again, woman. *Silenzio,*" Signore Regillus roared.

"*Vostro Onore,*" Gabriel interrupted, trying to restore a sense of order to the room.

"I have heard all I wanted to hear from either of you. I am aware of the rumours spread throughout this city about you and your bastard child. We know nothing of your past before you *happened* upon this fool." The councillor jabbed his finger at Bianca before sweeping his hand to include Gabriel in his edict.

"Your sentence, one with which my co-council are in total agreement, is immediate banishment from the city. I have instructed the guards to confiscate your properties and see you are escorted out of the gates *tonight*. Do not think of taking any of your harvest with you. Consider it compensation for the cost of finding a new doctor."

"But, Signore, my woman is mere days away from delivering—" Gabriel tried to reason.

"If there is any justice in this world, mother and child will die during the birth. Now, get out of my sight before I see to it myself."

Ice in her tone, Bianca vowed, "You will rue this decision." Turning her back on the trio, she marched to the door.

Catching up, Gabriel hooked his arm around Bianca, clutching her against him as she trembled with reaction. He feared the confrontation had taken its toll, hastening her labour.

"They will all pay, Gabriel... every last one of them," he heard her swear softly as he assisted her out.

5

The lights of Rome illuminated the horizon behind the pair as they struggled northwards. Gabriel had heard tales of a *guaritore* somewhere in the wilderness who might be willing or, at least, could be bribed to help deliver their child

Most claimed the woman was more witch than healer. At this point, Gabriel would take anyone he could find.

He felt Bianca's resolve weakening with each passing hour. The cold of the early autumn night had reduced her defiant tone to a pained whimper.

As the pink streaks of a new day painted themselves across the inky violet sky, Bianca collapsed. The first true pains of labour wracked her body, wresting a scream which echoed into the predawn.

Scooping her into his arms, Gabriel, not knowing whether they were going in the right direction, continued along the path Bianca had set them on.

That was when he saw the unnatural glimmer in the distance.

Ignoring the warning bells landing in his head, Gabriel

trudged towards the glow. As they approached, it became apparent this was not the flicker from a farmer's bonfire, nor the gleam from a villa's hearth.

No, these torches were on posts, towering over what appeared to be an encampment of caravans, bathing the wheeled metal boxes in a harsh glare Gabriel had not seen before.

His weary steps took him closer until he could distinguish details. The fluorescence from the torch towers, powered by an energy source alien to Gabriel, did nothing to enhance the aesthetics of the collection, rather it highlighted the various stages of wear and tear each caravan bore due to constant relocation.

Too late, Gabriel realised who these people were and, his protective instincts aroused, prepared to face off with the two guards who fell on him.

"Well, well, well, what do we have here?" He heard one guard remark, sounding almost disappointed. "The prey comes to the hunters. Where is the thrill in that?"

"Aye," his comrade agreed. "Takes all the fun out of the chase. Like we're reduced to vultures waiting for him to drop dead. Maybe if we spook him, he will run."

"He does not look intelligent enough to spook. Besides, with the tasty little morsel he is carrying, not sure—" the guard broke off in mid-sentence when he got a proper look at the woman in the stranger's arms. His face paled in recognition.

"Angelo, get the Padrona, now," The guard fired an order to his companion, who gave a confused nod and ran to the largest caravan, which sat in the heart of the camp.

He pounded on the ageing metal.

Muffled death threats and the odd aggrieved, 'keep it down, we're sleeping here', could be heard from the surrounding, wheeled hovels.

The light above the door popped on when it swung open.

Gabriel saw an older woman silhouetted in the doorway. Her shabby robe, cinched at the waist, struggled to provide her with a modicum of modesty.

The expression on her weathered face was not one of delight at being woken before the sun.

He watched the tip of a cigarette, clenched in the corner of her mouth, flare, while she brushed her fingers through salt-and-pepper hair, apparently sizing up the situation.

"This better be good, boy, or you will be tonight's game."

"*Mi scusi*, Padrona." Visibly rattled by the threat he'd just received from the camp's Mistress, the man, Angelo, begged forgiveness. Pointing an accusatory finger at the little huddle on the camp's edge, his voice quivered when he tried to explain. "Antonio told me to get you, Ma'am. I know nothing else."

Shaking her head, she pushed past Angelo, growling, "Why am I not surprised!"

The woman stormed to where Antonio waited, paying scant heed to the newcomers. "Antonio, before I ban both you and your good-for-nothing brother from my sight, why the fuck did you not have the balls to come get me yourself?"

Antonio's gaze lowered at the woman's rebuke. Wordlessly, he inclined his head at the unconscious female.

The sight was enough to douse the woman's rage.

She dropped onto the ground next to Bianca and began checking for a pulse. Her eyes bored into Gabriel, "Get her in my caravan, *now*."

The woman was on her feet and halfway across camp before her order registered with Gabriel. He did not need to be told twice and chased after her.

Negotiating the caravan's narrow doorway was awkward, especially while carrying Bianca. Ducking the best he could, he still smacked his head against the frame.

Swearing at both the door and his clumsiness, Gabriel finally made it inside.

The condition of the interior was no better than the outside, suggesting at one time this rolling villa had sat abandoned. The walls were a dull shade of piss yellow, the leather upholstery on the seats and benches was cracked and faded.

Nonetheless, there was ample room. A place suited to the leader of this band of nomads. Well, that and the collection of trophy heads, displayed meticulously on the wall opposite the couch where the woman was pointing.

"Get her over here. I am losing what limited patience I have for the likes of you being in my camp," the woman growled at Gabriel.

Trying not to bump into the matriarch, Gabriel laid Bianca carefully on the couch. Keeping himself between the two of them, he faced the old woman.

"I know who and what you people are," his voice was sombre, "but I have heard of your skills as a *guaritore*. You are the only hope I have to save my woman and our child," he paused, hoping his plea would appeal to her conscience.

"If offering my head for your wall as payment is—"

Gabriel's bargain was cut short by a coughing fit, triggered when the smoke from the woman's final drag on her cigarette was exhaled into his face.

Satisfied she had silenced the farmer, the woman crushed the butt into one of the innumerable ashtrays strewn throughout the caravan.

"*Vaffanculo*. I will decide whether you keep it. Now, shift your hulking great body so I can tend to my daughter."

"*Daughter?*" Gabriel echoed in disbelief.

"*Sì*," the woman grumbled. "And I should be grateful to you for returning her to her people... but her present condition prevents me from doing so." Arching her brow at

Gabriel, she elbowed him aside, repeating in a cigarette hardened bark, "Move your ass and let me see to my daughter."

Gabriel was unsure what surprised him more, finding out the truth about Bianca and accidentally meeting her mother, or being told by the old woman to go fuck himself with such vehemence.

6

_____

For the better part of four hours, a battle of wills ensued between the old woman — who introduced herself as Noemi — and Gabriel.

Whenever he inched closer to Bianca to let her know he was near, the woman growled and shooed him away with the same vigour *he* would dispatch a murder of crows from a cornfield.

It irritated Gabriel no end, but he tried not to interfere.

By mid-morning, Noemi had revived Bianca, which led to the latter's contractions quickening. It concerned Noemi's *guaritore* instincts at how close together they were. This was Bianca's first child; her daughter should be in labour for most of the day. By her calculations, the babe would arrive in less than half that time.

To make matters worse, the healer's greatest fear was coming to fruition. From what she felt, the baby was breech, and usually a sign the mother would be the one who died during the birth as the baby struggled to be born.

Masking her concern, she pinned her daughter's man, with a baleful gaze. "*Culo*, is this your doing?" she asked.

At the end of his tether Gabriel was fed up with the old woman's attitude, healer or not. "Look, witch, I've had enough of the insults—I have a name," his words tinged with outraged exasperation.

"And I am sure your dead madre was very proud of giving you it with her last breath, but I want to know if this is your child?"

It was Bianca who answered through the pain, "*Sì*, Mamma... it is Gabriel's... he is the only one."

"Then I need you here with my daughter to give her strength and keep her moving while I prepare a few potions." She tipped her hand towards her apothecary table. "I am not about to let either mother or child die, but we are all in for a long day."

Noemi gathered various plants from her shelf and spread them out on the table in readiness. With narrowed eyes, she watched Gabriel help Bianca circle the confines of the caravan questioning what it was about *this* male.

How is it, Bianca Ricci, that you, who showed zero interest in the opposite sex, despite the number of passably handsome men right under your nose, ended up falling in love with an outsider and a bloody farmer to boot?

I would have been happy to know you would assume your role as leader of the caravans with any of them... well, except Angelo and Antonio.

Returning her attention to her herbs, Noemi cleared her mind and concentrated on the task at hand. Whatever she might have wished for her daughter was irrelevant; Bianca had made her choice.

In her prior life, Noemi had been a medical researcher for one of the leading pharmaceutical companies in Italy. When the world went to shit, she had 'liberated' whatever medicines she could get her hands on from the laboratories and, eking them out, did her best to keep her family and friends alive.

Word about her healing powers spread and, before she knew it, people sought her help and skills, resulting in this ragtag encampment.

Regrettably, because so many required treatment, her supplies were quickly exhausted. Noemi's only option was to turn to the knowledge of their ancestors. After centuries of man grinding his faith into pill form, it was the unassuming plants of the Earth which saved them.

Similarly, prior to the catastrophic collapse of civilisation, doctors often rushed to cut the baby from its mother's womb without considering the consequences or looking for alternative methods of delivery. When the plague eliminated *skilled* doctors, there was no one properly trained to handle the sudden rise in difficult births.

Noemi had learnt the hard way how to get it right. Many a mother and child had died under her care, but trial and error had taught her the correct combination of herbs and natural remedies.

Although this reduced, significantly, the need to resort to a cesarian section in order for either mother or infant to be saved, the number who had *both* survived the birth could be listed on one hand. Noemi attributed the phenomenon to luck not expertise.

That said, a breech birth required the special touch of knowing when to pull the child and when to let the mother push. Otherwise, the baby would tear the mother apart.

Hoping to stave off any problems, Noemi started Bianca on a tea derived from a mixture of raspberry leaf and skullcap root to prepare her daughter's uterus for the birth. She hoped the elixir would also make Bianca's contractions more efficient and less painful.

Waiting for the tisane to take effect, Noemi busied herself

crushing together dry chamomile, rose, and lavender in her mortar. She added the mixture to one of her geranium essential oils to create a formula that would keep her daughter focused and calm throughout the next phase.

While Noemi concocted her potions, Gabriel helped Bianca shuffle around the furniture. By now, Bianca's contractions were minutes apart, she refused to move anymore and sat on the couch.

Looking up at the collection of mounted heads, she muttered, "I hope they find the surprise I left them."

"Bianca…?" Gabriel was perplexed

Bianca cried out as another contraction hit her. "Gabriel… if I die today… it was me."

Taking the seat next to her, Gabriel had no idea what she was talking about… or whether she was delusional from the pain. "I am sure this can wait, sweetheart, we need—"

"*No*, dammit," she burst out. "It cannot. You need to know. I took the fool doctor's head. I warned him not to touch me that way again but what did *he* do? He laughed… he actually *laughed*. That'll teach him, the oily snake is not laughing now."

His brain caught up with her words, and Gabriel felt heat suffuse his face. *His woman was capable of killing without remorse.* "Did you know the raid was happ—"

His question went unfinished.

Bianca gripped his hand as the next contraction made her double over and scream in agony.

Noemi yelled at Gabriel, "Help her get on her elbows and knees."

He did his best to get Bianca into the position her mother had ordered, his efforts hampered when she barged past to check on her daughter.

Dread and doubt beset Noemi when she discovered Bianca was fully dilated, and the bottom of the baby's feet were presenting. Noemi had seen too many die when this happened, uncertain her skills were adequate enough to deliver the child safely.

Bianca's distress snapped her back to reality. This was *her* daughter and grandchild. She would *not* fail them.

Resisting the urge to act too soon, Noemi encouraged her daughter to bear down. She was impressed to hear the big oaf who in his clumsy way was trying to be a support to Bianca, tell her how much he loved her and that he could not wait to teach their child the secrets of the vine.

Noemi rolled her eyes at the thought of her grandchild — apparently a girl from the portion of the baby now visible — *ever* wasting her time in a field.

It was not until Noemi spotted the baby's umbilical cord that she pulled in earnest. Slowly and nimbly, she worked each of her granddaughter's arms out, all the way to her tiny shoulders.

Panic assailed her when she reached up to guide out the new-born's head, to find the cord circling her neck. If she did not act quickly, the baby would be stillborn.

Grabbing a clamp from her medical supplies, she fastened it to the cord, then cut it, aware the lives of mother and infant were slipping away.

Once she had delivered the baby successfully, Noemi turned her attention to persuading her granddaughter to breathe. Using an aspirator bulb — something she had salvaged years ago — she purged the baby's nose and throat.

Giving a firm swat to the baby's butt, Noemi listened for the typical infant squalls. There was nothing, no sound at all.

The baby, limp in Noemi's hands was quickly turning blue. With no choice, Noemi initiated the resuscitation techniques she learnt when an intern, praying to whichever deity might be listening that her training was not in vain.

Bianca was begging to know whether her baby was alive or dead.

The sound tore at Noemi's heart, but she had to shut out her daughter's pleas to concentrate on encouraging, almost willing, the baby to breathe. About to give up, she heard the sucking gasp for air from the infant, followed by the cry of life.

Looking at the couple, tears streaked down Noemi's face for the first time in an age. She took a moment to savour it.

Cradling the screaming bundle, she waited for Gabriel to move Bianca into a more comfortable position before placing the babe in her daughter's arms. Watching mother and child bond, Noemi smiled down on them in maternal approval.

In this world, even more than the old, happiness always found a way of going to hell in a heartbeat.

7

B ianca's face leached of all colour and, as her body spasmed to rid itself of the afterbirth, she began to haemorrhage.

Noemi snatched two little bottles from her apothecary table. One contained angelica root to help Bianca deliver the placenta more easily, while the other was a concoction of Shepherd's Purse, yarrow, and witch hazel.

Using the dropper in the first tincture, Noemi placed a full measure under Bianca's tongue. Waiting a few minutes for the initial dose to take effect, she repeated the procedure. It wasn't long before the herbs performed their medicinal magic.

The problems did not end there. Noemi had to contend with Bianca's bleeding.

She encouraged Bianca to get the newborn to nurse. She could not remember exactly why, but she'd read about it in some book a lifetime ago and was willing to try anything.

In addition, she massaged around her daughter's uterus, applying the mixture from the second bottle to slow the bleeding.

Helplessly, Gabriel watched Noemi fight to repel the insidious embrace of death. He could not imagine a future without Bianca — not now — especially when the healer had just saved their daughter.

Noemi's determination paid off, and gradually, the bleeding subsided. She checked Bianca's pulse, satisfied it had the strength necessary to keep her daughter alive. For the first time in more seasons than Noemi cared to count, it was her application of hard-earned knowledge and expertise, *not* luck which resulted in the survival of mother *and* child.

"I must write that down so I can replicate it." She chuckled inwardly. "Maybe, just maybe, I've found the key to saving humanity from extinction."

Gabriel's attention was prised from Bianca, and his curiosity piqued when the Padrona began rifling through a cupboard. From the amount of clutter falling out, it was plain she had not checked this storage locker in quite a while.

Noemi tossed knick-knacks to the side, swearing she would force Antonio and Angelo to learn how to clean and organise her caravan. She was far too busy overseeing the camp to do it herself.

"Ah, here it is. Thank you, Giulio, for having the foresight to leave it with me."

Noemi withdrew an old sword from its scabbard. Years of neglect had not dimmed the sheen, the blade glinting in the late afternoon sunlight streaming through the windows of the caravan.

"This belonged to Bianca's father. He was a *Colonnell* in the Esercito Italiano before the fall. It was a gift from his *Generale di Brigata* when Giulio was assigned his first command.

Gabriel inspected the sabre. The pristine condition of the blade indicated it had never seen conflict.

He read the inscription to himself: *Presented to Colonnell Giulio Ricci 14 September 2019.*

Noemi's tone softened in reminiscence. "I want you to have it, so you have the wherewithal to defend my child and grandchild properly." She pointed to the pruning shears on his belt. "I doubt those would inflict a nasty cut, never mind a mortal wound... if you could get close enough to manage that."

"I could not accept such a precious gift..." Considering Noemi's earlier contempt, Gabriel was flabbergasted.

"Fool, a sword does no good unless it is bathed in the blood of your enemies. Take the damn thing and stop arguing."

"May I ask how he passed? Was it from the disease?"

Noemi inhaled a sharp breath remembering the chaos of those final days. They still possessed the power to shake her.

"I had just returned to work after giving birth to Sophia. Giulio and his brigade were ordered to defend the Roma Military Hospital against looters. They fought to the last man but were overwhelmed by gangs scavenging for drugs."

Before her emotions got the better of her, she changed the painful subject. "Since we appear to be family, maybe you should start by calling me Noemi."

Gabriel smiled and nodded.

Noemi was quick to add, "But, if I ever hear the word *madre* come out of your mouth, I will take that blade and collect your tongue."

⁂

After some food and a full night's sleep, Bianca felt almost human again. Sunlight filtered through the curtains, prompting a yearning to be outside, to fill her lungs with the fresh morning air. Her newborn daughter cradled in her arms, Bianca settled on the chaise, Noemi had ordered the brothers to set up in front of the caravan.

Comfortably swaddled in a warm blanket, she observed her surrounds, relieved the clamour of camp life did not appear to bother the child, who's disgruntled whimpering was not a complaint about the din, but a demand to be fed. Gladly, Bianca obliged.

As the infant suckled, Bianca hummed a tune, one she had heard her mother sing to her sister when Sophia was a baby, hoping she had sung it to her as well. Occasionally, she brushed a loving kiss to her child's head.

Bianca was happy to be back among her own. She knew her mother had worked miracles during the birth, keenly aware that, had she remained in Rome, it would have been a coin flip as to whether mother or baby lived.

Worse, following the demise of the city's only physician, regardless of who was to blame, the survival of either was unlikely.

Pushing that grim thought out of her head, she turned her attention to a problem neither she nor Gabriel could agree upon... their baby's name.

Gabriel wanted to call the child Isabel... after his mother. Bianca favoured Giulia... in honour of her father. Absently running through names in her head, she was distracted by the sound of something scraping across the gravel. Looking up, she saw Noemi dragging an old metal chair to join her.

"*Buongiorno*, Mamma. I hope we did not disturb you," Bianca greeted, with a smile.

The Padrona was surlier than usual. In part, this was due to lack of sleep. She had maintained a vigil throughout the night to ensure her daughter and granddaughter were no longer at risk. In the main, it was because she had forgone her habitual three cigarettes with her morning coffee, for the sake of the baby.

"Hardly, Bianca. Who could have slept with the snoring coming from the damned farmer? He was so loud, he drowned out the generator."

"That *farmer* is the father of my child, and he does have a name."

"So, he likes to brag."

"Besides, Mamma, you forget how often your snoring drove Sophia and me out of the caravan."

"Bah... whatever."

Noemi fell silent. There was a question she wanted to ask Bianca but could not think of a tactful way to phrase it. In the end she just blurted it out.

"What happened the day you vanished? If you tell me that man of yours rendered you unconscious to kidnap you, I will see he is drawn and quartered immediately, and his head tossed into the Tiber."

"Mamma, you will not touch him. Gabriel saved my life... and you should welcome him as your son."

"You dare speak to me in that tone?"

"*Sì.*"

The stern expression on Bianca's face, as she stood up to her, reminded Noemi of Giulio so acutely, tears pricked the corner of her eyes. She scrubbed at them as though removing dust, ridding herself of the momentary weakness.

With a resigned sigh, she implored, "Are you going to tell me the story, or do I continue to believe the lummox hauled you off and knocked you up?"

A red stain crept up Bianca's face and she averted her eyes, recalling how her own stubbornness had led to her current predicament. "You recall sending me for game that day?"

"Yes, it was early in the morning, so you should have been back no later than midday."

"That is true, Mamma, but I failed to find anything suitable to contribute to the meal." Lowering her voice, she confessed, "So I pressed on."

"Did you not see the clouds gathering?"

"I was sure over the next rise I would find something."

"Did you ignore everything I ever taught you, child? Why did you not turn back when the temperature dropped?"

"And admit to you I failed so simple a task?"

It was Noemi's turn for regret, as comprehension dawned. Her daughter had abandoned her better judgement in order to please her mother.

Bianca went on, "By the time I registered I had travelled beyond our boundaries, it was too late. The winds whipped up, turning a light snowfall into a blizzard. I became disoriented and couldn't find my way back. Gabriel found me near frozen to death in his field. Mind, Mamma, you would have been proud of how ferociously I fought him off before I collapsed from cold and hunger."

Speaking to the head of her clan, instead of her mother, Bianca added, "I beg forgiveness, Padrona, for my weakness. I deserved the banishment to the elements I received."

"Nonsense, *mia bebè*. The storm prevented the entire camp from looking for you, by the time it subsided, there were no tracks to follow. We had no way of knowing which way you had gone. We thought you had succumbed to the weather. Your poor sister was inconsolable for days."

As was Noemi, something she was not prepared to reveal.

There was no need. The grief etched on Noemi's face at their failure to find Bianca, was more eloquent than any words.

Her mother mustered up a smile. "We did have a nice send off for you. Nearly burned the camp down."

Bianca chuckled softly, "I am glad you restrained yourselves, that would have been a catastrophe. Where else would Gabriel and I have gone for such expert medical care?"

A weighty pause interrupted their conversation, each contemplating the 'what ifs'.

Persuaded that the stupid farmer had *not* harmed her precious daughter, there was one question which continued to nag Noemi.

"Why did you not return when you could?"

Bianca blushed like a lovesick schoolgirl. She brushed another gentle kiss to her sleeping daughter's head. "Gabriel would never have prevented me leaving had I chosen to but, that stupid farmer as you insist on calling him, is quite skilful when it comes to..." her blush went from pink to puce. "... well, your granddaughter should be all the answer you need."

8

An air of optimism bloomed during the subsequent days, the first few of which were consumed by rowdy celebrations of the birth. Countless bottles of appropriated wine — Gabriel noticed several from his own stock — christened the new addition.

To everyone's well-concealed surprise, their Padrona suggested the proud parents name their daughter Aurora. Initially dubious — the Hunters were not a sentimental bunch — it seemed fitting, especially as the tiny girl's arrival represented a new dawn in a world currently enduring an otherwise harrowing existence.

That she and her mother had survived the ordeal, encouraged the camp to believe the curse, which seemed to befall expectant mothers, might have been lifted. There was a renewed conversation amongst the women about how they might be willing to chance pregnancy — just maybe.

Amidst Bianca's continued recovery, and adjusting to the routine of a newborn, the relationship between Gabriel and Bianca strengthened. The couple was inseparable and doted on their child.

Gabriel never revisited Bianca's confession pertaining to the doctor's death. He placed what happened in Rome in its own epoch. The terrible events were easier to handle if he accepted, they had occurred in another time and a different location.

Even the tiny girl's usually churlish grandmother could not help but light up whenever she had the chance to steal the infant away from her parents.

The year ticked away. Winter loomed, encouraging the Hunters to top up their stores. Noemi, especially, knew how many ailments could strike during the colder months and took every opportunity to bundle Aurora into a wicker basket and tote her to the fields where she collected herbs for her medicines. She described the benefits of each root and leaf to the infant, certain she understood every word.

On one such foray, a beautiful and unseasonably mild autumn afternoon, Noemi had been so occupied teaching her granddaughter the benefits of dandelions, she let the afternoon slip into dusk without realising.

Gathering her things, she thought it odd the evening creatures hadn't begun their nightly chorus. Whimsically, she imagined they were delaying it so as not to disturb her granddaughter, drowsing in the basket.

Noemi hadn't reached the track before the truth hit home. A dozen Vatican guards converged on her, swords drawn.

"Halt, witch. By decree of the Roman Imperial Council, I am to take custody of the child," their captain stipulated, managing not to choke when he said 'Imperial', which always sounded ridiculous. He was loyal to his city but, privately, thought the title was a complete misnomer and only added to the councillors' already inflated egos.

"The fools in the city have no claim to this child. She belongs to our camp." Noemi retorted coldly.

"She belongs where she might provide the greatest good to the largest number," the captain contested. "Word has reached the city the child is imbued with magical powers. This can be the only reason she and her mother survived. The Council demands to know how it is so and how best to duplicate it."

"Magic? Are you daft? The only magic this child possesses is the ability to make people act irrationally."

"Hold your tongue," he bellowed. "The child... *now*."

In an effort to protect Aurora, and maintaining eye contact with the captain, Noemi set the bassinet between her feet on the grass. Straightening up, her fingers curled around the handle of the blade tucked in her belt.

"Away with you before you find yourselves additions to my wall." She brandished the lethal-looking dagger, letting them know her threat was not baseless.

"*Va' all'inferno,*" she shrieked when she saw they were not about to retreat.

The captain sneered derisively. "**Hell**, *puttana*? We have *all* been in hell for the past twenty years."

Like a wildcat, Noemi launched an attack. Cutting and plunging her weapon into any flesh which dared come too close. But twelve to one odds never end well.

The steel of the guards' swords tore into her body. Noemi's howls of pain, along with Aurora's wails, echoed across the fields, summoning the tribe to battle.

A cowardly blow from behind, severed the Padrona's head from her shoulders, ending her onslaught.

The guards stared down at the woman's decapitated body. One chuckled, while stealing her knife as a souvenir, "No more fitting of an end to the witch. Justice is served today in that she suffered the same fate as those taken by her blade."

Another suggested, "How about we throw lots to see who gets her head as *their* trophy."

The one who had struck the deathblow objected, "Oi, it was my sword ended her reign. By rights, it should be mine."

The thud of approaching boots curtailed further discussion. Hurriedly securing the distraught baby in the basket, one of the guards snatched it up and the men fled to the sanctuary of the city walls.

A sense of foreboding compelled Bianca's younger sister, Sophia, to run ahead of the rescue party.

Hearing her agonising scream of *"Madre,"* the rest sprinted to the path's edge where Sophia knelt sobbing uncontrollably next to her mother's brutalised body.

Gabriel assumed the unenviable task of convincing the weeping woman to supervise the conveyance of Noemi's remains back to the camp. He ordered Angelo to accompany her as extra protection and to ensure she did nothing to get herself killed.

The band stared as though Gabriel was speaking a foreign language, all harbouring serious reservations this farmer, prey no less, had any right to issue orders.

Their qualms vanished when Gabriel drew his sword and sped in the direction of the city, Bianca — *his woman* — and their new Padrona, on his heels.

Without hesitation, they followed.

The guards had rounded the first bend in the Tiber before Gabriel and Bianca reached the riverbank. Aurora's cries mocked their failure to reach her kidnappers in time.

Frantically, the parents began to argue about the best way to rescue their daughter.

Antonio was the first to catch up to the couple. The voices he heard were sharp, but they were not blaming each other. Rather, Bianca was pleading with her man to think of something... *now.*

Part of the last incursion into Rome, Antonio thought he could provide the solution.

Pacing off about a hundred steps from the narrow sandy bank, he came to the edge of a small thicket, where the Hunters had taken refuge while the guards conducted a perfunctory search. Choked with wild grasses and weeds, it had provided the perfect cover.

To Antonio's relief, he found the three small boats, Angelo and he had camouflaged, intact in the undergrowth.

He hollered for Bianca at the top of his lungs, "Padrona, *velocemente.*"

Bianca sped over the rough ground to where Antonio pointed. Spotting the boats, she threw her arms around him.

"I thought if we were successful once, better to be ready for the next time," he grinned diffidently.

In reality, there had been no masterplan to disguise the crafts. He and his brother had been too lazy to carry them all back to camp.

To be fair, Angelo *had* suggested they hide them in case the guards returned.

No need to admit that to anyone, Antonio thought. *Especially to the Padrona.*

"I shall reward you with an extra case of wine and my eternal thanks," Bianca praised effusively, "on the proviso you share it with your brother."

She had known the pair long enough to be aware it took both to come up with one cogent plan. But, at that moment, Bianca was thankful her mother had a soft spot for the brothers — even if she never showed it.

Noemi had found the two urchins scrounging through garbage cans for food. After spending a couple of days watching the two wrestle other beggars who tried to purloin their ill-gotten gains, she recognised their potential.

She used to tell Bianca, she depended on their brawn more than their brains. Tonight had proved their wit should not be underestimated.

The instant the others slid to a halt alongside the trio, Bianca signalled them to haul the boats into the river. Gabriel and she took point in the first one, waiting impatiently while the rest clambered aboard. Somehow, all twenty-seven squeezed into three craft built for half that number.

The trip down the Tiber was perilous. Not only was there the constant fear of being spotted by patrols but also, they had to contend with the water sloshing into the overcrowded vessels, increasing the chance of capsizing.

✦

They had not made it half a kilometre before excited yelling reached them from behind.

Cautiously, Bianca stood to see a rickety boat paddling desperately... and bailing... in their direction. It bore a group of the camp's teens, orphaned at birth.

While in training, each had demonstrated potential, but all were untested and ought to have remained behind as guards.

The three lead boats slowed giving the fourth a chance to draw level.

Bianca wanted to scold the rambunctious lot, but before she could, the eldest rose to his feet.

Bowing, rather drunkenly given the swift flowing river, he did his best to convince her they had made the correct decision. "Padrona, please forgive us for defying your command to stay in camp but, like you, we cannot cower in the corner of a caravan and allow others to risk their lives to avenge your mother's death."

The boy delivered their justification with as much bravado as he could muster in his young voice. He concluded respectfully, "She was our Padrona, too."

That none in the boat were sufficiently trained to be awarded their own swords was no deterrent. They had armed themselves with makeshift knives and clubs, which they held aloft in support of the boy.

"If you are done with your speech, quiet yourself and prepare for trial by fire. I hope the efforts of your teachers were not in vain." Bianca's curt reply masked the pride she felt for those in the leaky boat; it was not in the Hunters' nature to display emotion.

Looking over the mass of eager faces crammed into the four rowing boats, it occurred to Bianca, this was no longer a rescue and vengeance mission.

This was an all-out war against Rome.

9

————

While fortune smiled on them… the rapid current carrying them quickly, it also meant the city guards had made their way to the heart of Rome with equal speed.

The small flotilla beached upriver from the old Enel Green Power Plant. The abandoned station, Rome's onetime electricity source, had become the headquarters for the city's first line of defence against any intruders who decided to use the Tiber as an ingress into the metropolis.

From their vantage point, Bianca and Gabriel observed a handful of men policing the gantry which linked the plant's towers.

Running an eye over her modest band, Bianca chose five of their most skilled and waved them over.

In a hushed voice, she delivered her orders, pointing at their goal, "It's imperative for you to make it up to that gantry and eliminate this obstacle. Afterwards, you must hold this position to assure our escape."

With wordless nods, they pledged their lives to the Padrona.

With daggers drawn, the marauders made their way along the riverbank. The order to take a life was nothing new to this group. They had been raised not to question the need for a death. Each knew they would be rewarded handsomely for their deeds... as long as stealth played in their favour.

None challenged the copper-haired woman with the classic buzz cut who took command. Nicoletta had been schooled to do so from birth. Her father had served the former Padrona as her personal guard until his last breath.

Nicoletta being female was no obstacle to her father. He simply pushed her harder, his training regimen, pitiless. Most in the camp feared her.

Except for her man, Dante.

He was the only one, besides the Padrona and her family, who dared stand up to Nicoletta, and a voice of reason she heeded.

It took about fifteen minutes to reach their first objective, the power plant entrance.

While the others kept watch, Nicoletta jiggled the doorknob. Although locked, the glimmer from an interior light indicated someone was within. Pulling a cloth from her pocket, she wrapped the hilt of her dagger and quietly broke the glass panel in the door.

A wave of her hand over her shoulder brought Dante to her side. The two kicked off their boots before entering the building.

On silent feet, they crept along the corridor until they reached a corner. Both froze against the wall, shielded by the darkness.

The light, Nicoletta had seen through the glass, originated from the hallway beyond.

Peering around the corner, she saw a man — a warden or sentry she surmised — sitting at an old desk, apparently attempting to read some papers by the oil lamp hanging from a hook on the wall beside him.

Nicoletta was amused by the man's obvious irritation. *Stupid city dweller, the written word is wasted on your kind,* she thought sardonically.

The man succumbed to the futility of the exercise, tossing the papers on his desk. Two sheets floated to the floor. Tempted to leave them there, the sentry knew *his* commander would have his ass for setting a poor example.

Leaning to his right, he heard an odd shuffling and felt the icy sting of metal puncturing his skin.

Almost before this registered, the warden was dead, Dante's blade sinking into the base of his skull, piercing his cerebellum and severing his brain stem.

Against her inclination, Nicoletta paused their advance long enough for her man to claim what was rightfully his. In perverse fascination, she watched Dante unhook a hatchet from his belt to cleave the sentry's head from the rest of his body in one fell swoop.

"Do not think your prize is going over our bed, Dante."

"Then you better collect a couple yourself, woman," Dante scoffed. "I grow tired of looking at the ugly, old farmer who is hanging there now."

Ignoring his comment, she retreated to the entrance to collect her footwear and the other three of their party.

As Nicoletta sat on the floor to lace up her boots, Dante tossed a grisly sack in her direction. Instinctively, her hand shot out to catch the bag before it hit her.

"Not a chance. Your kill, your carry."

Nevertheless, she was clutching the bag when they

emerged from the building, aware those waiting in the boats would see her drop the bag by the door and judge it her trophy.

She hid a wicked grin. *Let them believe it is mine. Serves Dante right for attempting to transform me into his pack mule.*

The watchers below were sorely tempted to let out a cheer for the two; but congratulations for the kills would come later.

※

The warriors re-entered the plant, taking care to be as discreet about their presence as before. They followed the hallway, which led to a door at the far end, skirting the desk and the dead sentry.

Through the small square of wired meshed glass, a flight of stairs, presumably ascending to the next level of the building was visible. A pair of highly polished black boots appeared and vanished on the first landing, marking the path of a patrolling guard.

Dante checked the door handle. The knob refused to budge.

He threw the weight of his shoulder against the solid panel to force it open, another futile manoeuvre.

His lack of success demanded a closer examination of the door. The locking system included an engaged deadbolt.

Humiliation at not checking this, plus Nicoletta's glare burning into the back of his head, elicited a muttered, "Fuck."

Nicoletta, who had been leaning against the desk during Dante's abortive attempt, did not bother to hide her conde-scension, and pointed to the corpse at her feet.

Despite her faith in her man as a fighter, she was keenly

aware that his current euphoria, resulting from his gruesome kill, meant Dante had neglected the obvious... frisking the deceased.

Crouching, she patted down the body thoroughly, digging through all the pockets in the process.

In one, her fingers snagged a keychain clogged with an absurd number of keys. She dangled them at Dante, disappointment and anger marring her face.

Dante's response was a sheepish shrug.

Nicoletta flipped him off and continued her search. It was worth the effort.

Normally, the sentry's holster would be devoid of any sort of weapon and used only for appearance. Tonight, it held a loaded pistol.

Nicoletta hated guns. It meant the one wielding it was too cowardly to fight fair. However, her personal battle morality didn't matter. Now, it was vital they breach the gantry, and help save the Padrona's child.

The 9mm was not unknown to her. Her father had seen fit to include firearms as a staple of Nicoletta's childhood. That was until bullets became a gratuitous luxury for the inhabitants of the encampment, and the time spent hunting for them, wasteful.

Removing the magazine, she discovered fifteen rounds in the clip awaiting her orders. Snapping it shut, she released the safety and drew back the slide.

Keys and pistol in hand, she passed her companions, batting a flirtatious wink at Dante.

Holding the pistol while locating the correct keys was cumbersome, forcing her to present the grip to Dante to hold it temporarily.

"Don't you even think about pulling the trigger," she warned.

"Never, my love."

She rolled her eyes at him.

Her hands free, it did not take long to find the deadbolt key. The manufacturer had the foresight to engrave their name on lock and key. As for the knob, that was a matter of trial and error.

At the fifth key, the knob clicked free.

Retrieving the pistol, Nicoletta charged up the stairs to the first landing.

Before any of her men could ascend, two random bullets whizzed down the staircase to strike Ettore who was right behind Dante. Clutching his chest, the fatally wounded warrior slumped to the stairs, drowning in his own blood.

Dante heard return fire and the thud of a body collapsing to the concrete, followed by the clang of heavy boots ascending to the next level.

With no time to grieve for Ettore, Dante grabbed the handrail, and hauled himself around to the landing, expecting to see Nicoletta bleeding profusely. To his abject relief, the lifeless body belonged to a second sentry.

The echo of gunfire propelled Dante up the stairs. By the time he reached Nicoletta, she was at the head of the stairs next to the door leading to the gantry and two more guards lay dead in the stairwell.

Waiting for Dante to join her, Nicoletta checked the ring for the key to the gantry door. Peeking through the glass, she studied the guards gathered at the far end of the walkway, seemingly oblivious to the carnage which had occurred on her side of the door.

Sensing the presence of her mate, Nicoletta held up three fingers in a tacit reminder that she was now in the lead.

His quiet retort burst her bubble. "You know the rules.

Taking a life with anything other than a blade does not count."

Meaning the three in the stairwell would retain their heads... and she trailed Dante.

As she pointed to the key poised in the lock, Dante heard her mumble something under her breath. Though he could not hear exactly what it was, he was sure it was something he was anatomically incapable of doing.

He shook his head and exhaled a muffled chuckle.

Assuming a stance reminiscent of a pirate from some aged fable, Nicoletta positioned herself with the pistol in one hand and her blade in the other. She nodded at Dante to unlock the door.

The pair charged through, the remainder of their boarding party on their heels, taking the sentries completely unawares.

Nicoletta emptied the magazine at the advancing guards, pinning them down as her men prepared for battle. Both sides converged at the middle of the gantry.

The riverbank reverberated with the clash of steel during the resulting melee.

It was impossible for Bianca and Gabriel to distinguish whose bodies were being hurled into the Tiber but, as quickly as the skirmish was initiated, it ended.

The observers could not discern any movement above them.

For one heart-wrenching moment, Bianca feared she had lost a fifth of her loyal contingent. *And for what? Had they at least dispatched the guards as they sacrificed their lives?*

The exultant smile which spread across Gabriel's face, along with him jabbing his finger at the bridge, veered her attention to the gantry.

. . .

Standing at the railing, Nicoletta used a severed head as a gruesome signal for the rest to proceed.

"Don't you think this trophy is more handsome than that wizened thing you collected?" Nicoletta teased Dante, who joined her to watch the boats glide soundlessly beneath them.

Triumphantly, the couple waved at their comrades, receiving a flurry of excited grins and waves in acknowledgement.

"Knife-fight to determine who gets to mount their trophy?" Dante challenged.

"No sulking when you have to look at him every night."

10

One hurdle cleared. Gabriel knew they were fortunate to make it inside the walls of Rome unchallenged but, from here, it was essential to meld with any traffic which might be on the water at this time of night... not to mention avoiding detection by the patrols.

Landing upstream from Castel Sant'Angelo, Gabriel guided the group along the path which flanked the Tiber to the flight of stone steps leading to the Ponte Sant'Angelo and the adjacent Castel.

While Bianca had become familiar with much of the city's layout during the previous year, she was grateful to have a man by her side who had lived there his entire life. Until tonight, she had no clue this path, or the steps existed.

Pausing far enough up that they were concealed from any patrols above them, Gabriel risked a quick peep over the stone embankment. It disturbed him to see the frontage of the Castel oddly deserted.

The booths along the outer wall of the fortress, which

normally served as market-stalls, looked as though they had been abandoned in haste.

With no one in sight, Gabriel gave the signal for the troop to ascend the last few steps and make their way to the Castel's main entrance.

A peculiar sight halted them. The doors, typically closed at this time of night, stood wide open and unattended.

Bianca tapped Gabriel's shoulder. Her unspoken caution, unnecessary when he twisted to look at her. Both were contemplating the same reality... they were walking into a trap. What choice did they have but to trip the wire? The life of their child was at risk.

Bianca assessed the group behind them. It was impossible for such a large number to enter unnoticed.

No tactician, Gabriel had drawn the same conclusion. Rubbing his chin, he dredged his brain for ideas. Suddenly, he had a brainwave.

Downstream from their position, perched in the middle of the river, and connected to the city by two bridges, sat Tiber Island.

Local legend held that the island was created when Tarquinius Superbus, a hated tyrant was driven from power and the citizens of Rome threw his body into the river. His body sank to the riverbed, causing the dirt and silt to accumulate around it, eventually becoming the foundation of the island.

Throughout antiquity, the locals avoided it, only sending the worst criminals and the contagiously ill there to perish.

Now, Tiber Island supported the skeletal remains of the deserted Fatebenefratelli Hospital. When Rome's population plunged to its current levels, the demand on the city's numerous medical institutions also diminished.

It came as no surprise to the general public when the elites elected to house their considerable arsenal in the hospital. They certainly did not want to keep the explosives in their own backyard.

The recent rise in the river, resulting from a series of storms in the north, meant any boat would be able to land virtually at the former hospital's doors.

⁂

The memory of the chaotic streets, choked with citizens fleeing to the Vatican at the mere thought the Hunters were still inside the city walls, played into Gabriel's plan perfectly.

In a low voice, he laid out his course of action, much to the amazement of Bianca.

"I need six of you to remain with us. The rest will divide up and continue down the Tiber. One boat will land on the northern tip of Tiber Island, the other two will continue on to Ponte Sublicio…"

He spent the next few minutes outlining his strategy, as well as a timetable for when each component needed to be accomplished.

Bianca who had grown up and trained with most of their party was confident she could delegate specific tasks to the appropriate member. She assigned Dante's younger half-brother, Dario, to lead the strike on the armoury.

To a stunned silence, Bianca selected Antonio to lead the second attack on the residential sections of Rome further down the Tiber.

As Gabriel concluded his plan, Bianca realised he had overlooked a vital part.

She hailed Rosa and Viola, the youngest of the orphans.

Taking them to one side, she asked, "Can I depend on you two to execute a crucial piece of this assault? I seriously doubt any of this will come to fruition if you fail."

She detailed what she expected of them if they agreed; that it required no small amount of guile and all the speed their legs could carry.

Rosa and Viola accepted the challenge without a second thought.

Before helping the girls into their respective boats, the Padrona thanked them for their bravery. "Tonight, you are Furies who will avenge my mother's death. The city will tremble at the sound of your voices."

Before sending them on their way, Bianca touched each of the leads on their shoulders for luck.

Noemi's voice echoed in her head, "It would be a waste of breath, my child. What could you possibly say to make their pending deaths any less painful?"

⁂

The trio of boats were relaunched into the Tiber and, in tandem, made their way downstream.

They rounded the bend, pleased to note the blazing torches dotted around the grounds of the former hospital illuminated their first objective nicely.

Reaching the tip of the island under the Ponte Garibaldi, Dario leapt into the chilly, deep river. Treading water, he waited for one of his comrades to lob him the line tethered to the bow.

Due to the higher than normal water levels, it was Dario's responsibility to guide the boat safely over the submerged concrete reef Gabriel had warned him would be there.

When his knees scraped against the rocky slope, Dario steadied himself, then followed the incline to the cement plateau. The high tide provided just enough clearance to land the craft.

Safely ashore, he drew his blade from its sheath and waved Antonio to their next targets, seeing the two boats vanish into the night as he helped the rest disembark.

Dario thought the plan was feasible but suspected, because of its intricate nature and the need for perfect timing, they would all be dead before the moon set. The Padrona's expectations might be extreme, but to contradict or oppose her, never entered his head, nor indeed any among them.

Squinting in the moonlight, Dario surveyed the building. The farmer had instructed him to locate the entrance to the morgue. In keeping with the island's folklore, the guards in the armoury shied away from this area, believing it to be the sanctuary of the dead. It was rumoured that any who ventured inside, never returned.

While Dario did not fear the dead — he had slain enough to make him impervious — he was also a pragmatist.

The superstitious fools were more likely to have met their demise by falling through rotten floorboards than at the hands of evil spirits.

The others joined him, and the motley crew crept up to the rear of the hospital. As Gabriel had advised, they came to a large sliding door, secured by a rusty padlock, but unattended. A few solid whacks from the pommel of Dario's blade smashed the lock.

The door groaned in agony as its rollers were forced along the track to open it. The stench of formaldehyde wafted out to greet them.

Advancing beyond the reach of the torches outside, Dario bumped into a large solid object. Running his hands over it, he worked out it was a wooden table, draped with a sheet.

Grasping it by the edge, he turned it on its side. He had

been tempted to flip it over, but they could not afford to draw attention... not quite yet.

Dario located one of the table's legs and, with the assistance of one of his band, snapped it off. Tearing the sheet into shreds, he wrapped them around one end. Further scrutiny revealed a bottle of rubbing alcohol, which he used to saturate the material, then lit the makeshift torch.

At his feet, a mass of human bones in a confused heap next to the overturned table. Swinging the torch in a slow arc, Dario saw the entirety of the morgue was filled with similarly sheeted tables.

His friend, Rolando, touched him on the shoulder. "This is a bad omen, we should not be here."

"Come now, Rolando. We used to play catch with their skulls as children. What harm can come from a handful of covered bones?"

"Do not mock, Dario. Mark my words, no good will come from this night." Rolando reiterated.

Dario had never heard Rolando speak in such morbid tones. He already had a sense of dread for this operation. *Did Rolando feel it too?*

Without another word, he crossed to a door at the far side, on which the word *uscita* in faded green letters was still distinguishable. *According to the farmer, this should be the door leading to the main part of the hospital.*

Before venturing into the passage, something impelled him to lower the torch. His unspoken theory, a frustrating reality. A hole, about two meters long, swallowed up the corridor.

11

A glint of something metallic emanating from the depths of the void caught Dario's eye. He angled his torch to expose the remains of an unfortunate patrol spread out over the concrete floor below.

With a wry chuckle, he lectured those behind him. "This is what happens when you are a lazy city dweller. You grow fat enough to break floors."

Dario examined what was left of the hallway.

Rolando suggested, "There's enough space between the hole and the wall to edge across... I think."

"Then, my friend, you first."

Rolando frowned at Dario, before doing as instructed. Flattening himself against the wall, he inched around the hole, cautiously. The supports under the floor creaked with each step, but, miraculously, held.

Reaching the other side, Rolando shot his friend a superior look. "I don't have all night," he challenged.

The rest followed Rolando's route. The last man, Benito, tossed the torch Dario had entrusted to him across the gap before attempting his balancing act. The latter picking it up before the chill tiles snuffed it out.

They padded along until they came to an adjoining corridor, spying torches at the opposite end beckoning to them.

Dario shrugged. "I guess we go this way."

Quietly, they proceeded down the long corridors which led, inexorably, to the heart of the building. At each open doorway or dark alcove, they expected to be confronted by soldiers stationed here.

They had yet to see any sign of the munitions the farmer had assured them were stored in this godforsaken dump.

Running out of time and patience, Dario growled, "This is what we get for listening to that simpleton. We should have stormed the Castel as originally intended."

In hopes of convincing Dario to persevere, Rolando coaxed, "Let us check the next—"

A bullet silenced him, fragments of skull and brain matter showering Dario who watched his friend crumple to the floor. Rolando had been his companion since childhood, more a brother than his own.

In an instant he was gone... felled in this ludicrous plan.

Incandescent with rage, Dario — his blade drawn — charged along the passage in the direction of the gunfire, lobbing the torch in front of him to illuminate his quarry. Bullets whizzed passed him, one tore into his shirt sleeve, ripping a gash in his bicep. The pain went unnoticed in his adrenaline fuelled fury.

Reaching the man with the pistol, Dario heard a *click*... but no discharge of the cartridge expelling the slug.

In fear of the advancing lunatic, the guard had emptied his clip, erratically. Before he could replace the magazine, the steel of Dario's sword sliced through his chest, to protrude out of his back.

Dario had no intention of taking this bastard's head as a prize. He did not want to see the prick who had snatched Rolando from him.

He had a better use for his victim. Using the dead man like a screen, Dario continued his onslaught, his fellow warriors joining the fray.

After impaling another soldier, Dario discovered, to his chagrin, that he could not extract his sword from his human shields, forcing him to leave the blade lodged in his victims.

Picking up the sentry's rifle, he wedged himself behind a column and returned fire.

He heard one cry out, "Stop shooting you fool. Do you want to send this place to the moon?"

"Death holds nothing for me... can you say the same?" Dario spat. "Drop your weapons or face your eternity."

The clatter of guns hitting the ceramic tiles echoed along the disused corridors of the once bustling hospital.

"Now, come out with your hands up."

A troupe of men, young and old, edged closer to the Hunters' position. Fingers laced behind their heads, and fear etched on their weary faces, all were certain, one way or the other, their deaths were imminent.

Dario had no time for a harvest.

"Show me where the armoury is and then skedaddle before I take the lot of you."

A sentry with a white bushy beard, his stripes signifying him as the ranking officer, pointed to a large room previously designated, if the wooden plaque by the doorjamb was to be believed, as a chapel. "I-It is in there... what's left of the stockpile."

Dario fired a bullet into the man's skull in retribution for Rolando's death.

"The rest of you, get the fuck out of here."

He watched the dead man's subordinates flee to the nearest exit, committing the direction they took, to memory.

It was not that he was feeling magnanimous in sparing their lives. During the foray into the building, and subsequent melee, he had lost track of their escape route.

❁

The invaders entered the armoury, and came to a halt, eyes gleaming in the flickering torch light. Munitions lay everywhere; from the altar at the far wall, barely visible under numerous haphazardly stacked boxes, almost to where they stood.

In the sentries' hurry to defend the place, they had cracked open cases of rifles and their matching ammunition.

Passing out the weapons, along with loaded clips, a reluctant smile slid over Dario's face, and he decried his lack of appreciation for the guards' assistance. "I feel remorseful, I neglected to thank them for their foresight in opening the crates for us."

The sarcasm in Dario's voice, made his companions chuckle, convinced it was impossible for him to feel *anything*, attributing his berserker offensive to his reckless nature.

Dario let them believe that.

To his dying day, he would never speak of how Rolando's death had consumed him with grief and the overwhelming desire to have his own life ended. He banished the memory of his friend's murder to the furthest reaches of his mind.

Spotting several waterproof munitions satchels hanging from a row of hooks, he snatched one and flung it over his shoulder.

While the others stocked up on automatic rifles, Dario

71

and Mirabella combed through the crates for the ones containing the items they had been ordered to retrieve.

It was Mirabella who stumbled over them... literally... her boot smashing into the old wood.

Teasing Mirabella on her catlike reflexes, Dario finished what she had started, and wrenched open the crate, filling the canvas bag with the explosives he found therein. "I dare you to dance by the fire when we return," he taunted, and suffered a punch to his shoulder for his cheek.

Satisfied, he and his crew had gathered what Gabriel wanted, Dario pried open a box marked *Bastoncini di Dinamite*. Inside, he found forty sticks of TNT. The faded, red paper around each stick attested to their age, and possible instability.

Gingerly retrieving one of the sticks, he attached the equally ancient blasting cap and fuse. Easing it back into the case, he spooled out the wire behind him as they scurried from the building.

He had never played with explosives before, and had no clue what might be considered a safe distance... especially bearing in mind what was at the other end of the fuse.

Shrugging, in indifference rather than concern, Dario lit the fuse. He watched it begin to sizzle its way to the chapel.

"Sleep well, my friend," Dario murmured to Rolando.

The group ran at breakneck speed to where they had moored the boat. They reached it in time to untie the rope and row to the middle of the Tiber before they heard the first explosion.

The second sent a fireball, and the majority of the hospital's upper floors, skyward. The shockwave overturned the little craft.

What had seemed a great idea at the time, turned out to be disastrous because the weight of the extra weapons around the necks of the passengers dragged them underwater.

The added burden of the satchel Dario had filled in the armoury, sucked his strength, but his survival instinct kicked in, and he fought upwards. His lungs screaming for air, he broke the surface of the river, and swam to the western bank, somehow clinging to the stolen rifle.

Exhausted, he lay on the grassy shore, gasping for breath. His ears rang with a fortissimo clanging which muffled all other noise. Confused, he wondered whether it was Rome's innumerable bells, perched high in their lofty towers already ringing a warning.

That this was possible in the few minutes since detonation, never entered his head.

He rolled to his side to check who else had made it. He could only see Benito and Mirabella, both of whom had managed to keep hold of their newly acquired guns.

A twinge of sorrow pinched Dario's chest. Presumably, the rest of their comrades, along with their weapons had joined Tarquinius Superbus at the bottom of the Tiber, forming an accidental honour guard for the legendary tyrant.

Dario noticed something dark trickling from Mirabella's ear. Carefully, he touched it, making her jerk in surprise.

He glanced at his finger. It was streaked with blood. *What the hell?*

Tentatively, he repeated the gesture on his own lobe. Stroking the delicate shell, he understood the cause.

The concussion from the blast had been powerful enough to rupture their eardrums.

He muttered, knowing neither of his two comrades could hear him, "As if we don't have enough to contend with."

12

Antonio stood in the middle of the Ponte Sublicio looking south, listening intently for any sign that Dario had completed his part of the mission.

Originally, it had been recommended, he face the opposite direction in order to witness the sky lighting up. Given nobody knew how many tons of explosives the armoury held, nor the radius of the resulting damage, he gauged it prudent to turn his back on Tiber Island.

The only sound he heard was the approach of the city guards.

A haggard voice called out, "You there. Why are you abroad at this time of night?"

Pretending he hadn't heard, Antonio locked his gaze on the river below. Two boatloads of Hunters, prepared for a fight, watched him intently, waiting for the word.

Hoping to mitigate any needless loss of her people, Bianca had stipulated they anchor behind one of the bridge's support columns, using it as a natural blast wall.

"Are you deaf?" The guard quizzed, loudly — just in case

this lunatic was, in fact, deaf. "You know the city is under a mandatory curfew. State your business or face arrest."

As a child, Antonio had heard tales about people throwing themselves into the Tiber rather than tackle a future, which appeared desolate at best. The Padrona had used them as lessons to teach the brothers how certain emotions diminished the less resilient until the only escape was to take their own lives. A weakness which, she insisted, continued to afflict those who clung together behind the city walls.

Her advice rang in his ear as though she stood right next to him. *Use it to your advantage.*

"Stop," he shouted at the guard. "P-Please do not c-come any closer."

Antonio did his best to mimic his pathetic city dwelling prey. He had heard enough of them beg for their lives during Hunter raids inside the walls, though to use the same words now left a bitter taste in his mouth.

His comrades below stared in curious silence as he tried to ad-lib his way out of the situation.

The plea failed to halt the guards, and the patrol commander ordered, "Move to the centre of the bridge and drop to your knees."

"I warn you, if you come any closer, I'll jump to my death."

This brought the group to a standstill.

The city's elite did not give two hoots for the average citizen of Rome, *but* there was always some anonymous bureaucrat hidden away in the Castel who would magically appear when this idiot's body washed up, demanding sundry reports, in triplicate, chronicling the incident in fine detail.

The commander gentled his tone hoping to talk the crazy man into changing his mind, and not prolonging his shift. "Why would you want to waste your life so senselessly?"

Antonio spun about to glare at the man. "Senseless you say? Did it make any sense that my poor, dear brother was taken from me by that band of damned, dirty killers?"

Flinging himself against the concrete railing, he winked down at the sea of insulted faces in the boats.

"And why did they kill him, you ask? Just... do you hear what I say... for sport, a way to satisfy their perverse blood-thirst, that is why."

One of the marauders below whispered to his comrade, "Think anyone would mind if I killed him? *Sport? Perverse bloodthirst?* Does he even know what that means?"

Antonio decided to end his charade with flair. "Alas, if I cannot see my brother in this world, I will look for him in the next!"

Exasperated by the would-be jumper's antics, the commander offered, "Look, it is late and neither of us wants to be on this bridge. How about we go and find a drink and you can tell me what drove you here?"

"What purpose would that serve?" Antonio demanded and perched on the rail of the bridge, one foot on the capping. "I'll still want to die in the end. Except, I guess, I'll be drunk and unable to feel the sting of death claiming my body."

Antonio was impressing himself with his dramatics. Those in the boats struggled to muffle their laughter.

A flash in the northern night sky, followed by a thunderous explosion, rocked the bridge under those standing on it, bringing them to their knees. Antonio who, thankfully, still had one foot on the bridge otherwise the plan might have ended quite differently, fell sideways to sprawl on the concrete path.

Stunned, the guards' attention swung in the direction of the sound, to witness what appeared to be a large portion of the northern horizon on fire.

Antonio had no need to admire the display. Scrambling to his feet, he gave the signal those in the boats awaited. The two craft separated, one to either side of the bridge where the crews disembarked.

Though Antonio wanted to spearhead the attack on the Testaccio side of the river, the mass of guards, trying to assemble in confusion, blocked the eastern end of the bridge. Forced to change his plan, he waved the leader of the orphans in that direction.

Spinning on his heel, Antonio fled to the opposite end. As the pursuing guards came off the bridge, Antonio's men surrounded the guards and cut through them in short measure, grumbling their displeasure at being denied the honour of collecting trophies.

While Gabriel's annoying order forbidding such endeavours resounded in their heads, they, grudgingly, accepted that to delay, even a moment, could ruin everything.

The battle over, the Hunters made haste to their next goal — Trastevere.

Torches at the ready, the invaders fanned out into the over-populated streets hugging the Tiber. It was not lost on them that the surrounding apartments were constructed of brick and mortar due to the city's fiery past.

This made little difference to what was about to happen.

Shattering windows as they made their way through the streets, the groups tossed in burning torches, setting ablaze curtains and furnishings.

Flames spread rapidly through the lower floors of the buildings, driving residents into the street.

This was where Rosa and Viola came in. Viola, the faster of the two, had been sent to the Testaccio side of the river.

Her job was to herd the Romans towards the Tiber, while Rosa, her partner in crime, incited fear into the inhabitants of Trastevere.

Lagging behind the others until a sufficient number of buildings were ablaze, Rosa and Viola began screaming at the top of their lungs, "Run, run for your lives. The Hunters are in the city. Get to the Vatican."

As the fires began to take hold in the buildings, the girls' cries were multiplied exponentially by the chorus of victims clamouring to get out of their houses and to the Vatican for sanctuary.

Viola succeeded in her task more efficiently than any had anticipated. Once clear of the Ponte Sublicio, she glanced over her shoulder to see it clogged with people, their valuables in hand.

In disbelief, she watched the mob stampede over bodies, while some, not moving fast enough, were heaved over the edge of the bridge headfirst to get them out of the way.

Dozens lost patience at the snail's pace to which the crossing had slowed and decided to risk swimming across. Others turned north in search of an alternative route.

Unbeknownst to anyone — including the invaders — unless people were prepared to risk a lengthy trek, the only viable bridge for those on the east side of the Tiber was the very same Ponte Sublicio from where the attack had commenced.

This highlighted the Council's disastrous blunder in demolishing a number of the secondary and tertiary bridges which used to span the river, for the sake of scavenging building material... and controlling their citizens' access around the city.

The five-hundred-metre blast originating from the armoury had torn free the span of the Ponte Garibaldi to the north of Tiber Island. Both the Ponte Fabricio and the Ponte Cestio were reduced to dust and had crumbled into the river.

The victims raced to the one remaining bridge close to the island, the Ponte Palatino. Their initial relief that it appeared to have survived the blast was quashed when it became clear, the entire north-facing side had evaporated.

A foolhardy few scaled the southern railing. A handful succeeded, encouraging more to follow. The weight proved too much for the damaged support and it too crashed into the river.

Witness to their neighbours floundering in the Tiber, many fled further north to the, hopefully secure, Ponte Vittorio Emanuele II.

13

While the districts along the banks of the Tiber, south of Ponte Sant'Angelo, were about to be catapulted into chaos and destruction, the northern reaches lay blissfully oblivious.

After Bianca and Gabriel watched the three boats glide beneath the Ponte Vittorio Emanuele II and disappear around the first bend downstream, Bianca tapped her man on his shoulder. It was time for their group to step into what they anticipated would be an ambush. One for which they were prepared.

Given they were wearing sturdy boots, the eight people creeping through the gates of the Castel Sant'Angelo employed unprecedented stealth to ensure their advance went unheard. As they passed under the curved lintel of the darkened doorway, Gabriel suppressed the gruesome notion that they were stepping into the gaping maw of a hungry giant.

All those weeks ago, when the couple was ordered to convey the doctor's body to the old cells, they had taken the normal path to the left and round the building. About to follow the same route, a peculiar metallic rattle and the low hum of voices had them spinning on their heels.

Puzzled, Gabriel lifted a finger to his lips. He knew there was a way to access the large so-called garden, which circled the Castel, *but who would be using it at this time of night?* The public had been barred from enjoying the space years ago, and the erstwhile moat had been reduced to a gravel courtyard.

Garden? Deserts had more grass.

A subdued glow revealed the doorway, indicating it stood open. Curiosity got the better of him and, keeping in the shadow of the wall, he padded quietly to the door.

He chanced a quick look, only to be faced with what appeared to be a lengthy barricade of thick shrubbery blocking the way out. He frowned at the obstacle. *What the hell was the point of such a ridiculous partition, right at the entrance to the garden? Why did they want to prevent access? What were they hiding?*

On closer examination, Gabriel ascertained it was more decorative hedge than impassable barrier, but the vicious-looking thorns adorning the bushes would be an effective deterrent to the unwary.

This did not answer the original question. What was the strange clinking?

Parting some of the branches and getting scratched for his pains, his gaze fell on a sight which answered all his questions and instigated a diversion to the main plan.

He retraced his steps to find the rest of the group fidgeting impatiently. More than one grousing about putting their trust in a damn farmer.

"What are you doing?" Bianca hissed in exasperation. "We don't have time to play tourist."

"You need to see this," he replied in undertones, and

something in his voice doused any objections. At the door, he pointed at the peculiar obstruction.

"We cannot go around, we will be spotted. We must go through. It will offer protection, but watch the thorns," he warned as the invaders crawled through the shrubbery, the barbs ravaging even the smallest area of exposed skin.

Concealed in the deep shadows thrown by the foliage, they watched in shocked silence as the bulk of the Guardia Cittadina Romana d'élite completed what had obviously been a training exercise.

Returning to formation, the soldiers stood to attention, their backs to the Hunters. Here was the *crème de la crème* of the city's defenders, normally assigned as security detail for the Council and the Vatican.

A formidable foe at the best of times, tonight this unnaturally soundless drill added to their menace.

Despite the gloom of the garden, Bianca noted the soldiers were dressed in black instead of their standard military garb. She remembered her mother calling this type of uniform, riot gear.

Matching black helmets protected their heads and, if her mother was right, their faces would almost certainly be hidden behind black masks and full-face visors.

Whether this was the case, Bianca could not tell because the battalion had their backs to her.

Neither were they wielding their usual swords. Tonight, they were armed with automatic assault rifles.

Gabriel had heard stories about these weapons but, as far as he knew, no one outside the Guardia Cittadina Romana had even seen one, let alone had the chance to handle one.

The rarity of replacement parts and ammunition for these rifles, had prompted the Council, by decree, to limit their use to extreme emergencies. Shrouded in secrecy for two decades the sinister-looking firearms had transformed into an almost a mythical weapon of the gods.

The couple exchanged a look of awe at this deadly arsenal, as the commander walked along the neat rows of soldiers, inspecting his troops. This was no ordinary drill.

Glancing impatiently at the southern sky, Gabriel grumbled under his breath, "Dammit, what is taking them so long?"

Bianca laid a scratched hand on his, being the voice of composure... a first for her, "Give them a bit more time, Gabriel. What you have laid out is complex at best... and near impossible at—"

The blast from the armoury going up, shattered the silence of the courtyard, drowning out the last of Bianca's words.

It mattered not what she might have thought of the plan, pandemonium was about to cripple the city and before long the streets would be filled with a terrified populace, among whom the Hunters could effect their escape.

In unison, the guards spun around to witness the remains of the fireball lazily swirling its way to the moon.

Anxious eyes swivelled to their captain for orders.

Unmoved by the explosion, or his men, the captain forbade them from breaking ranks.

Aghast, Gabriel was confused that the billowing blaze had not caused the troops to disperse at speed, to discover the source.

For all in the Castel, it felt as though time itself was as frozen as the formation.

An eerie sound drifted on the still air. Indistinguishable at first, it increased gradually until cries for help could be discerned, at which point, the guards' hesitation vanished.

Their tactics were working, they were actually working. Bianca's heart swelled with pride at the efficiency of her people and their willingness to carry out Gabriel's plan.

Hearing strident pleas to an implacable commanding officer, the observers had no doubt some of the homes in the path of the flames belonged to these men — and their families.

The ranks broke when the captain refused to act.

He yelled for his men to return to formation, but his exhortation fell on deaf ears. Forced into action, and in a demonstration of his commitment to hold his position, the captain barked a single instruction to the remaining guards.

"Open fire on those cowards!"

This led to more men deserting, determined not to be responsible for the massacre of their friends.

The consensus being *those who ran were only trying to protect their families.*

The garden erupted in a blaze of gunfire at the hands of those who complied with the captain's orders. Figures illuminated like deadly auras with each flash of their rifles' muzzles. The gut-wrenching shrieks of the dying, along with the bullet-riddled bodies of the dead, filled the night.

Until recently, empathy was foreign to Bianca, but living with Gabriel had changed her... if only slightly. She wanted to protest at the senselessness of what had occurred. Although life had become just another commodity, even *her* people did not kill their own.

You defended them at all costs.

Gabriel clapped his hand across her mouth, stifling the scream he knew was boiling within her.

Perhaps recognising the futility of his actions, the captain gave the order to cease fire. The blood-curdling sounds of slaughter echoed into the distance, dying away in a faint wail.

The guards who perpetrated the massacre, found themselves staring down the gun barrels of their compatriots who had refused to participate and somehow survived the barrage.

The ensuing battle between opposing sides was briefer than the first, though equally deadly. By the time the smoke cleared in the courtyard, barely a handful clung to the land of living.

Warily, eight Hunters emerged from the obscurity. The prospect of liberating rifles and spare clips from some of the victims, too good to ignore.

Without comment or order, Gabriel and Bianca led their group through the fallen soldiers strewn across the gravelled rectangle, ending the lives of those lingering at death's door. This was the closest thing to an act of mercy the Hunters could offer.

The small band back-tracked, going around rather than through the prickly bushes. Bearing in mind their extra cache of weapons, it made no difference time-wise, but a great deal of difference to their battered skin.

Silent as phantoms, they slipped into the interior of the Castel. There was a child to rescue.

※

Time was of the essence. Each of the eight grabbed a torch from the sconces on the curved wall and followed Gabriel into the fortress and up to the Council Chambers.

The arduous ascent via the ramp and narrow ancient staircases, tested the strength of the fittest among them. Sweat poured down faces with each flight, hearts pounded in synchronisation with the rhythm of their boots thudding against the stones; urgency trumping stealth.

Gabriel was disconcerted by the lack of sentries. *Even if the Council deemed it impossible for intruders to breach the doorway to the Castel, they would still require protection to carry out whatever deed they had planned for Aurora.*

He arrived at doors to the chambers, panting heavily. They appeared ominous under the flare of his torch. He tested the knobs, only to find them locked, reinforcing his belief the ignoble triumvirate cowered on the other side.

Over the racket of those thundering up behind him, he bawled, "Stand clear."

Raising the automatic rifle, he pulled the trigger. Nothing. The weapon failed to replicate the spectacular rain of destruction, which had dazzled them scant minutes earlier.

"You useless piece of shit," he growled in disgust.

The touch of a hand brought his attention to the woman behind him.

Bianca smiled. "Allow me?"

She took the gun, pulled back the bolt to load the chamber and then flipped off the safety. Noemi had been an endless source of lethal knowledge to her children.

Returning it to Gabriel, she extended her hand to the door. "Now try it."

His finger curled around the trigger, and the rifle sprang to life. The antique wood splintered around them in a violent shower as the bullets burst from the barrel in a steady stream.

Gabriel paused firing to give the door a solid kick. The lock failed in its mission, giving way with a loud *crack*.

As the doors fragmented inwards under the pressure, Gabriel and the others swarmed into the chambers...

...to find them as dim as the rest of Castel.

The room was devoid of people, including their daughter.

14

Discovering their quest had failed, Bianca broke down. The stress of losing her daughter, and registering their efforts might have been for nothing was too much even for her to weather.

Uncaring that this was a sign of weakness she begged Gabriel for answers neither had. "Wh-Where is our child? Gabriel, what have they done with her?"

Embracing his mate, Gabriel felt her body tremble. It seemed her indomitable strength was abandoning her. As lost and frustrated as Bianca, he had no words of reassurance, making do with a compassionate kiss on the top of her head.

Momentarily, Bianca relished the comfort of Gabriel's arms drawing strength from him, then stiffened and pulled away to scan the room, with contemptuous eyes.

"This..." she swept her hand in an arc, encompassing the building and the city beyond its walls. "...is all echoes and illusions. Echoes of a past no one recalls yet yearns to rekindle. A past which encouraged those savvy enough, or crazy enough to assume dominion over the rest of us, but whose power is naught but an illusion. The first real challenge and poof, it has vanished, like the dawn's mist under the rising sun."

Gabriel stared at Bianca, her poetic turn of phrase catching him off guard. He was about to respond when she reverted to her usual sarcasm.

"Or just a bunch of spineless autocrats, wielding fear to keep the rest of us submissive."

He swallowed a chuckle, ushering her from the room, trying to mask his desolation at failing to find Aurora. A glimmer of light, which was not from their torches, filtered into the corridor adjacent to the chambers.

Gabriel glanced through the small lead window, and realisation dawned.

At the end of the Via della Conciliazione, in the elites' sanctuary, the torches burning in the Vatican piazza had transformed it into a beacon.

Tapping Bianca on the shoulder, he pointed. "There, my love. Our child is there."

Hurrying to the windows, Gabriel flung one open, enabling the couple to see the surging mass of humanity blocking the streets, all the way back to the Ponte Vittorio Emanuele II.

Even from this distance, the uproar apparently unfolding at the far end of the Via della Conciliazione was cacophonous.

The multitudes bearing down the broad street had come to a halt, doubtless prevented from entering St Peter's Square by the massive iron fence which spanned the entrance to the Piazza Papa Pio XII. The very one erected by the Council in its early days for added protection.

Gabriel imagined the sentries on the other side were praying the gate was strong enough to withstand the strain.

Their prayers would be in vain.

The rattle of gunfire from somewhere along the broad avenue sent the throng into a panic, and they rushed forwards.

The fence was no match for the weight of the city's populace. So loud was the boom when the great chain securing the gate snapped like a tattered string, the watchers in the Castel heard it echoing over the ruckus.

A tidal wave of people, desperate to get to the comparative safety of the basilica, ran headlong and without consideration for their fellow man.

Gabriel and Bianca stared in horror.

The guards, along with anyone who could not match the pace, would be crushed underfoot... probably to death... in the resulting free-for-all.

"Dario's handiwork, no doubt aided and abetted by Antonio's mob," Bianca posited as she viewed the madness from above. Comprehension chased across the faces of the rest, unable to see what Bianca was seeing, but they made no comment, it seemed... crass.

Gabriel gathered Bianca flush to his body, her back to his chest. "Let's go get our daughter."

❦

In the confusion, none of the citizens noticed eight strangers inserting themselves into the stampeding herd.

Now she knew where the Council had taken Aurora, Bianca surmised the best way to access the inner sanctuary was by blending in with the Romans, mimicking their erratic behaviour until Gabriel and she got close enough to slip inside the basilica unnoticed.

However, this did not come without its own measure of danger. From every angle, hands and elbows jarred them painfully, jostling the group as people tried to get past them.

Even though they were heavily armed, and somewhere in the crowd Dario and his men were following with their own weapons, Bianca ordered her unit to resist the temptation to discharge their guns into the frenzied mob.

"Not yet," she yelled. "We have neither the ammunition nor the time to waste."

It was not her soldiers she had to worry about.

From behind the red granite obelisk, towering above the centre of the Piazza San Pietro, gunfire broke out. The shooters were not aiming for the Hunters... their bullets sprayed indiscriminately into the flood of citizens.

It was a frenzied effort by the Vatican guard to prevent people from reaching the doors leading inside St. Peter's Basilica and disturbing the proceedings the chief councilman had described as essential to the survival of the city.

Bodies dropped around the Hunters. The crowd scattered, seeking shelter behind any available cover.

No longer hidden within the masses, Gabriel and Paolo, a man he knew in passing, returned fire at those trying to use the soaring Egyptian needle as a shield. A monolith, Gabriel had always thought to be out of place among the ancient architecture of Rome, and would not be upset if it fell under gunfire.

The duo pinned the shooters down, while the remainder of their group spread out to flank the sentries.

Bianca led the attack from the left, executing any who crossed her line of sight. Before the pincers could close on their enemies, ending the battle, she heard one of the automatic rifles, from the exposed portion of the piazza to her own left, go silent.

Under a fusillade of bullets from the few remaining Vatican guards, Bianca could not chance averting her eyes even for a second to see whose gun was out of ammunition.

The unfamiliar bursts of three new weapons quickly

replaced the other two, restoring cover to both teams, allowing them to converge on the obelisk.

The men behind the tall stone attempted to surrender, knowing they had no hope of defeating the armed band.

Regarding them as undeserving of quarter, Bianca strafed the lot.

The last sentry flung his weapon on the ground and fled for the doors of the basilica, only to be cut down before he reached the first flight of steps.

The gunfire subsided leaving Bianca free to turn her attention to where Gabriel had been.

Running across the piazza, she saw Dario and two others standing guard around whoever lay on the ground. Dario did not seem to be aware of her approach.

Fearing her man had been taken from her, she screamed at Dario, "What happened? Is anyone hurt?"

Dario did not respond.

15

"How dare you ignore your Padrona? Answer me now." Pushing past Dario, Bianca glared at him, not noticing his shock at being shoved aside.

He touched his ear trying to explain that since the explosion, he and his companions could hear nothing but a constant ringing.

Bianca was too preoccupied to pay him any heed.

Hearing her voice, Gabriel looked up.

In his arms, the lifeless body of Paolo. Blood stained the man's shirt and Gabriel's hands. "I-I do not know what happened, my love. My gun jammed, and before I got it to release, he jumped in front of me. He sacrificed himself for me. Why?"

Bianca knelt alongside the two.

Placing a hand on Paolo's stilled heart, she murmured an inaudible *Thank you*. She shook her head. "I wish I had an answer for you. Perhaps nature is changing."

This was not the moment to argue philosophy.

Bianca patted Gabriel's shoulder, promising, "A discussion for another day, love. We have more important matters to attend to first."

Conceding her point, he eased Paolo's body to the ground.

Picking up his fallen comrade's rifle, Gabriel turned to Dario. "Did you bring the explosives I—?"

Frustrated no one was listening to what he was trying to make them understand, Dario yelled, "Enough. I can barely hear either of you." He gestured to the other two. "And do not bother with them. They are as deaf as me."

Dario was sorely tempted to hit Gabriel with the satchel but, the way the night was progressing, that virtually guaranteed the bag would mysteriously explode, blowing them to smithereens across the classical piazza.

Handing the bag to Gabriel, he quizzed — somewhat sarcastically, "You *do* know what this stuff is, don't you?"

Gabriel nodded as he examined the contents.

"Then tell me, farmer…"

Dario's derogatory tone provoked a jab to his ribs from Bianca's elbow, which he ignored.

"…how are you aware of such things?"

Gabriel retrieved the package of plastic explosive, along with the detonator, his reply as condescending as Dario's question.

"Have you not noticed the massive brick thing circling the city, *Hunter*—?"

Dario saw Gabriel's lips moving but could scarcely make out what he was wittering about. "And? Get to the point."

After compressing the block, essential for what he had in mind, Gabriel inserted the blasting cap. "The walls surrounding Rome were constructed from the remains of former buildings. We used this stuff to bring them down in a controlled fashion."

With that, he pelted across the piazza and up the

sweeping staircase leaving Dario gawking idiotically, still baffled as to what on earth the farmer had said.

Bianca caught up with Gabriel as he put his shoulder to the Filarete Doors — in recent years, the sole entry point for the public and even then only in dire circumstances — to see whether they would open. Watching intently, she held her breath in faint hope they could forgo their original plan.

A possibility neither believed…

… and thus, their disappointment was minimal when the doors refused to budge.

"Please, stand back, *amore mio*," Gabriel adjured.

"No, not until you do."

"Then run when I tell you."

Exercising extreme caution, Gabriel managed to slot the armed explosive into the narrow gap where the two doors met, a handspan below the centre, then rolled out the wire.

In times of previous assaults, the citizens were granted refuge inside this building. While his compatriots congregated near the doors, Gabriel had relished the opportunity to explore the interior of the basilica.

During one incursion, he had studied the reliefs engraved on the door. He had no idea who or what they represented, but the images were similar to those which stared down at him from the high corners.

More importantly, Gabriel had spotted the thick bronze batten which secured the doors to their frame. He was not sure whether it had been part of the building's original construction, or whether the Council had added it later.

No matter the reason or history of the bar, the knowledge of its placement was of greater importance.

Confident in his assessment, he lit the fuse. Grabbing Bianca by the arm, he yelled, "Run."

Thankfully they had descended the three flights of steps before the explosives detonated, affording them a modicum of protection, but the blast knocked them to the ground. The intricately carved bronze doors slammed inwards violently, then swung back with similar force, sagging on their hinges.

Stunned and winded, Bianca sensed movement. Rolling onto her back in preparation for a violent altercation, she saw the unruly mob resuming their rush to the basilica and its now open doors.

Getting to her feet, she gesticulated wildly to capture the attention of her forces. She pointed at the rabble, yelling, "Keep them away from the doors, but avoid taking any more lives... if you can."

Under the renewed sounds of weapons being fired into the air and down into the grey stones of the piazza, Bianca pulled Gabriel to his feet. The two bounded back up the stairs.

Their goal... the nave.

As they ran through the entrance, Gabriel noticed the crosspiece had been sheared in two, each bronze door clinging stubbornly to its half.

Slowly, rifles at the ready, the couple made their way down the nave to the far end of the cavernous edifice, passing row upon row of empty chairs.

Hitherto when the city was invaded, the ruling body had arranged to have them set up to form an area within the basilica where those requiring refuge could rest while they rode out the brutal offensives.

Tonight, these same chairs, conspicuously empty, reflected the Council's decision to force the people of Rome to fend for themselves.

Treading cautiously to where the torches burned brightest, Bianca saw winged creatures atop an immense carved bronze canopy — ghosts of a forgotten faith.

Where once they acted as a magnet for believers, tonight they were powerless spectators to the obscenity being perpetrated beneath them.

The pair reached the ornate rail of the *confessio* — the semi-circular space leading to, among other things, the tomb of St Peter — and stopped dead.

On the high altar where popes had prayed and blessed the sacrament, lay their baby daughter, about to be sacrificed for some reason neither parent could fathom.

At the far side, the detested trio.

A crooked smile broke over Signore Regillus' face when he saw them enter.

"Ah, if it is not the happy couple. It pleases me to have you as witnesses. The science of man led us to the brink of our own extinction, which can only mean a form of witchcraft protected mother and infant through birth. It's time to find out what it is.

"*Puttana*, farewell your child. What I do, I do for the good of the city."

Bianca screamed, "I beseech you, *Vostro Onore*, have mercy on our child. It was not magic that saved h—"

"Your pleas, as well as your respect, are a waste of breath," he interrupted and raised the knife preparing to plunge it into Aurora's chest.

Without warning, gunfire reverberated throughout the sanctuary.

Bianca emptied her rifle above the heads of the autocrats, taking care not to hit her daughter. She gained a morsel of grim satisfaction when the three men dropped behind the altar for protection.

Tossing Bianca his weapon, Gabriel darted around the balustrade, and scaled the steps surrounding the altar in three strides to pluck their squalling child from the marble slab. "Take the head of the first one who pops up," he yelled, then realised she was already in position.

Hugging Aurora against his chest, Gabriel ducked when shots rang out. Looking over his shoulder, he saw one of the despicable executives sprawled across the floor, a neat hole in his forehead. "Serves you right, you bastard," he spat.

For the briefest instant, Gabriel met and held Bianca's frantic gaze.
Oh, how he loved her beautiful ebony eyes, he could happily drown in their velvety depths.
His chest pinched, *this is where our story ends.*
Thrusting their daughter into Bianca's arms, he mouthed, "Go."
With a nod, she sped for the door, sure Gabriel was in close pursuit.

The clash of steel from behind indicated otherwise.

Spinning around, she watched as her one true love, the man to whom she had sworn her life, drop to his knees trying to ward off the two remaining councillors.

Bianca's heart demanded she go back to him, but the cries of their daughter, safe in her arms, propelled her onwards.

She flew along the nave and out through the great doors, where she collided with a soot smudged Antonio.

"Padrona, it is impossible for us to hold back the hordes

any longer. Please, we must leave, now," he begged, steadying her.

"No, Antonio." Bianca kissed her daughter, then entrusted the infant to his care. "Get Aurora back to the camp, and see Sophia takes care of her. I cannot abandon Gabriel. Go."

Before Antonio could stop his Padrona, she had disappeared back into the basilica. Gesturing to the rest of his tribe, they fled the burning city.

16

For the next two days, the camp tried to keep their hands busy and their minds occupied, while they waited for Gabriel and Bianca to return.

After giving Rosa and Viola a lightning course in basic first aid, Mirabella pressed them into service tending to the wounded. The two youngsters continued to prove their worth, and Mirabella was confident they would become proficient Hunters.

They mourned their dead, even though only three bodies were recovered. Noemi, Ettore — killed at the power plant, and Paolo — who Dario refused to leave behind after losing his best friend and most of his team in the armoury. They became a symbol of those who gave their lives during the onslaught.

A huge pyre was constructed, and the wake lasted until the early hours. Everyone agreed, *after* their hangovers had diminished to a dull hammering, that the send off had been fitting.

The raid, though successful in that they rescued Aurora, had severely thinned their ranks and, not prepared to relax their guard, Dante and Dario had organised three shifts of four men to patrol the perimeter around the clock.

In the privacy of the Padrona's caravan, Sophia and Nicoletta argued about Sophia's determination to search for Bianca and… she conceded reluctantly… the damned farmer.

"Just give it one more day, please," Nicoletta coaxed. "Dario says it was utter chaos. They could easily be lying low until the furore dies down."

Sophia glared at her friend, her frown softening when she spied genuine concern on Nicoletta's face. "Fine," she capitulated, "one more day, but if they are not home by first light two days hence… owww, *fu…*" she bit off the expletive when the needle pricked her finger for the umpteenth time.

To blend in as one of the city dwellers, Sophia was sewing a cream-coloured woollen tunic. Hopefully, the smattering of blood stains on the fabric — testament to her battle with the needle — would give it a 'worn' look.

Their vigil continued…

…in vain.

Under the grey light of the waning half-moon, and with a silent apology to Nicoletta for reneging on her promise, Sophia made her way to the riverbank.

As she tugged on the gunwale of one the boats which had conveyed her people to and, thankfully for most, from their various points of attack, Sophia's fingertips throbbed. A reminder of the pain she had endured throughout the creation of the tunic, and how often she had pledged to sacrifice it to fire before its completion.

For the entirety of the hated exercise, Sophia, who was raised to be a fighter and would serve as security for her sister — when Bianca assumed reign of the caravans, had raged at the piece of clothing, "You damn, *pezzo di merda,* I was never supposed to be a seamstress."

Undeterred by her misery, Sophia was determined to launch the boat, and sail it down the Tiber into the city.

The going was slow and arduous. She stumbled in the sand again and again, unable to secure her footing, refusing to admit defeat. Even if it meant breaking her back in the process.

With another five meters to go, Antonio emerged from the brush.

He had followed Sophia since she slipped out of the camp but deemed it wise to stay hidden and out of her way. The sight of her stubborn struggle with the equally stubborn craft made it impossible to remain concealed.

"Padrona—"

Sophia's head snapped in his direction. "Do not address me as such," she hissed. "That is Bianca's title, and I know my sister still lives. I feel it."

Antonio drew a breath, asking softly, "And what is your plan for rescuing her, Sophia? Storming Rome by yourself?"

"If it were that simple, I would be in the heart of the city at this very moment, razing what is left of it."

Antonio pushed by her to grab the bow of the old boat.

"Well, you'll never make it at the rate you're going."

With all the strength he could muster, he closed his eyes and began hauling. After waging a fierce battle against the inanimate object for position, Antonio was positive he had reached his goal.

With a smug expression, he opened his eyes, set to proclaim his victory. Only to find he had gained no more distance than Sophia.

He did not look at her. Her sarcastic applause filled his ears.

"My hero," she scoffed. "What *would* I have done without

you?"

"How about I punch a hole in this damn boat and let you drown out there?"

"If it meant you could get it into the water, I would take you up on the offer."

Muttering to himself, loudly enough for Sophia to hear, Antonio snarked, "If it meant getting it into the water... I will show you, woman."

Spitting on his hands, he rubbed them together. Focusing his concentration, he gripped the wood and heaved.

This time it slid smoothly over the sand, nearly running Antonio over in the process.

Triumphantly, he declared, "See, I told you I could—"

"Keep your mouth closed and keep pulling," Antonio heard a familiar voice yell.

Gaping slack-jawed at the stern, he saw Angelo and Sophia pushing from behind. Huffing in disgust, Antonio did as commanded.

Before long he was knee-deep in the cold river. Knowing better than to complain, he held the craft steady to allow Sophia to board.

Retrieving a bundle, she had placed on a nearby log, Sophia tucked it under the seat at the stern. Climbing in, she made herself comfortable on the centre bench. Lifting the oars, she settled them into the oarlocks.

Antonio piped up, "You are not going alone, Sophia."

"Do you reckon I would be safer with you by my side? I am sure your face is being used by the city guard for target practice as we speak."

"Then take him," Antonio nodded at his brother.

"I would stand a better chance if I surrendered as soon as I reach the shore," Sophia grumbled.

"Padron—" Antonio was silenced by a face full of water flicked up from the oar's blade.

"Please, Sophia, at least allow me to row you downriver," Angelo implored. "If you believe I will impede your progress, I will guard the boat until you return."

"Fine," Sophia acquiesced with a groan. "If we waste any more time bickering, the sun will be up before we set off."

Begrudgingly, Sophia relinquished her seat to Angelo. Moving forward to the next bench, she stared in the direction of the smouldering city.

While she knew the brothers were only looking out for her best interest, she was determined not to acknowledge their concern.

Being indebted to others leaves you vulnerable.

A warning her mother had drilled into her from childhood. A favour owed needed to be avoided at all costs.

Repayment for so burdensome an obligation tended to outweigh any value in the original service provided.

Sophia sent a silent apology to Noemi, "Forgive me, Mamma, for being a disappointment thus far. Please, provide me with the strength I need to find Bianca."

Neither occupant spoke throughout the voyage along the Tiber.

Angelo wanted to ask Sophia what she had in mind by heading into the city, but she kept her eyes fixed ahead. With the loss of her mother and sister, it seemed... precipitous, prompting Angelo to question whether she was rushing to join them.

While facing one's enemy in a pitched battle — especially in the name of vengeance — was seen by their people as an honourable way to die, Sophia had other things in mind, even if it were only half a plan.

She listened to Angelo's steady oar stroke slicing through the water, the rhythm oddly soothing, allowing her to lose herself in her thoughts. With a clear head, she began brainstorming.

Opening her bundle, she double checked Bianca's city residency pass was safely within. A twinge of something — guilt perhaps? — pestered.

Sophia, left behind while most of the Hunters waged war against the Romans, fought her own battle with her subconscious, which insisted on presenting her with worst case scenarios.

Rather than waste her energy pacing the camp, or twiddling her thumbs, Sophia had cleaned her own caravan before moving on to her mother's. Halfway through her self-imposed chore, she came across a box of Bianca's personal items.

Swallowing her surprise that Noemi had kept such trivial trinkets, Sophia rifled through the contents. Spying the pass, she had pounced on it... *a very useful commodity*, she had thought, tapping the card on her chin.

When the others returned without Bianca and her man, Sophia began to devise a way to enter the city, the residency card, an important part of that plan. If nothing else, she could discover their fates.

Besides her disastrous attempt at sewing the tunic, she had managed to fabricate a crude smock, characteristic of those worn by field labourers.

Being able to pass as one of those farmers is key to gaining entry.

The boat slid past what had been the bustling village of Settebagni. A string of charred buildings at the edge of the river, marked the spot where Sophia had decided would be the opportune spot to be dropped off.

"Angelo, land over there." She pointed to what in a

previous life, no doubt, had been thriving businesses.

"Are you insane, Sophia? At least let me get you through the river gates, they're not much further."

"Which of us is crazy? Do you really think the city is going to allow any unidentified vessel to come within half a kilometre of that entrance? No, my friend..." Sophia smiled and brandished the purloined pass. "...I plan to walk through the gates of the city."

Angelo snatched the identity card. Scrutinising it, he had to admit there was a definite resemblance between Sophia and Bianca, despite the almost five-year difference in their ages. His biggest concern was the blatant forgery of the name.

Sophia had all but obliterated the name on the card. She had folded it over numerous times, making sure to grind it against the dirt and stones around the camp.

Angelo waved the gate pass. "*I* can see the similarities, but I know you both. Do you think it's good enough to deceive a sentry?"

She plucked it from his fingers. "They will when I show up at the gate in labourer's gear. Who would deny access to a poor woman fresh from the field?"

"And if they look close enough to make out Bianca's name?"

Pulling a small blade from her boot, she reassured, "I'll use this instead."

Not satisfied with either of her plans, Angelo grunted.

Sophia was out of the boat and making her way up the bank when the bow dug into the loose gravel of the beach.

He called after her, "You are about half an hour's walk to the nearest gate."

Something she already knew. Without turning, she retorted, "Then I'd better stop wasting my time talking to you and get a move on."

17

Coming to the first building atop the bank, Sophia pried open the precariously hung door. The screws holding the jamb to the last of its hinges gave, and the door landed on the wooden floor inside with a smack.

Cautiously, she poked her head through the frame. The floor appeared to be secure, though the walls showed signs of the fire which had ravaged its interior.

Risking one step, Sophia examined the remnants of the building's previous life. Along one wall were rows of small, metal cages, covered in soot and rust.

Closer inspection revealed the cages contained the bones of small animals. She guessed most belonged to dogs and cats, but some she was unable to identify because they were burned beyond recognition. An unfamiliar twinge of sorrow whispered at the sight.

"I hate being sent out here to the wastelands."

An irate male voice, accompanied by the clatter of boots at the front of the property, brought Sophia to a standstill. *It was barely dawn, someone was keen.* She heard him call out to his comrade who must have been outside. *Two someones.*

"Damn it, Nero, will you stop dawdling? I want to get finished here before breakfast."

The thud of a second pair of boots joined the first.

"For the love of mercy, Mauro, I needed to take a leak."

"Then you should have just pissed yourself. Can we get on with this?"

Sophia heard them shuffling at the other side of the wall. Retrieving the blade from her boot, she crept to the door connecting the two rooms and, thankfully, ajar.

Leaning against the wall, Sophia peered around the corner to see a pair of soldiers conducting a token search of the place.

She listened intently in hopes of gleaning information on the fate of Bianca... and Gabriel.

"Does the captain honestly believe those psychos would be hiding so far outside the city?" Sophia discerned the vexed question came from the second man, Nero. "I doubt that ass has ever been out here himself."

"Enough. You are giving me a headache with your whining. Nobody forced you to join the guards."

"Oh, I beg your forgiveness, Lord Mauro. But I would wager my belly hurts more than your stupid—"

Unconsciously, Sophia shifted to get a better view. She might weigh only eight stones, soaking wet, but it was enough to cause the board beneath her boot to creak loudly. She flattened herself against the flimsy partition and froze. *Dammit now she couldn't see them.*

The duo stopped in their tracks, and Sophia imagined they were facing the same door behind which she was hiding.

"Did you hear something?" She heard Nero hiss under his breath.

The sound of a sword being drawn from its scabbard was the only response to reach Sophia's ears, but who's, she could not tell.

Straining to catch the slightest confab between the pair, she detected a measured footfall. An advance interrupted frequently as though the owner kept pausing to listen for any other noise.

She contemplated retracing her steps but what if others waited outside the back door? Her only option was to confront them. Her shrewd gaze fell on a convenient crack in the wall. With a soundless sigh of relief, she squinted through it and saw the two men.

Confident she could dispatch Mauro with relative ease, she was concerned about his partner. Nero's rapacious expression resembled that of a Hunter in the throes of harrying unsuspecting prey, leading Sophia to surmise his excitement at the idea of a battle had sexual undertones.

Sophia switched her scrutiny to Mauro. His whole bearing was that of a man who wanted nothing to do with what might lurk beyond the partially opened door, preferring that Nero take the needless risk.

A sudden breeze hit the storefront, causing the structure to shudder and groan.

Assessing the rafters with a worried eye, Mauro ordered, "Time to leave. We are chasing shadows. It is nothing more than the building preparing to fall on our heads."

Nero's angry, "Bullshit, you coward. You heard the noise as clearly as I did. It is *not* the wind," evidenced his frustration.

"And I outrank your scrawny ass. I am commanding you to leave this place."

"But—"

"But nothing. We are out of here. If anyone is foolish to be hiding back there, I am sure they will perish with this decrepit building. Besides, if we do not return now, we will miss morning chow."

Through the narrow split, Sophia saw Nero glance over his shoulder, doubtless vacillating over the best course of action.

"Sheath your blade." Mauro's tone brooked no argument.

Nero grumbled something Sophia could not make out, as she watched him comply. He stormed past Mauro and disappeared.

Mauro also shot a final look at back of the building, before following on his comrade's heels.

The last Sophia heard was Mauro saying, "You should thank me, boy. If you ever ran into one of them, your head would end up as a hat rack on one of their walls. Trust me, I've seen it happen."

⸙

Sophia remained rooted to the spot until her legs began to cramp from the awkward position she had assumed to prevent the floorboard squeaking.

Satisfied she was alone, she stretched her aching limbs then, gingerly, crossed the floor to her discarded bundle. Each step felt like she was balancing on pins and needles.

Replacing the blade in her boot, Sophia inspected her field frock, debating whether to dust it off from where it had lain on the dirty floor.

"Why bother?" she chuckled. "Dirt suits my purpose."

She wrestled to drag the badly sewn garment over her head and, in doing so, snagged the material on a nail sticking out of the wall. The resulting jagged tear adding to the credibility of her disguise.

Satisfied with her impoverished appearance, she crept

through the building and out into the Via Salaria, the main street through the township.

Every business along the road had suffered the same fate as the one she had exited. Each was gutted and bore the tell-tale signs of an intense fire.

On her right, the ruins of what she considered to be *the* most peculiar attraction. A collection of the vehicles which used to clog the roads and, according to Noemi, spewed out toxic fumes, polluting the air.

Sophia's nose crinkled as she read the miraculously undamaged red and gold fascia — *Museo dell'Automobile*. The gleaming machines, once the pride of their owners, appeared to have been rammed through the plate glass windows onto the forecourt and torched.

While Sophia suspected her people had been blamed for the senseless destruction, she also knew so petty an act was beneath them. Aware the Hunters had not been involved in any altercations in this suburb, there was only one logical conclusion.

The perpetrators of the blaze, probably wayward teens with little else to do, had come from within the city walls — almost certainly the over-indulged offspring of the wealthy. Children from poorer families who spent every waking moment working in the fields, would not squander their precious free time on something so pointless.

"*Bastardi*," she bit out savagely, and turned south to Rome.

18

S ophia joined the purpose-built footpath which had been erected alongside the huge wall circling the city. Designed to provide the sentries an easy link between gates, it was also a popular short cut for the locals.

It was quiet at this hour of the morning and Sophia reached the Tiber in minutes. After listening to Nicoletta and Dante, she had realised the bridge connecting that section of the wall was the one which ran parallel to the power plant the Hunters had secured, three days and a lifetime ago.

Once across the river, she hastened to the gate on the Via Flaminia, originally part of an ancient and bustling trade route. Today it was less travelled but, located in walking distance of the cattle grazing pastures adjacent to Labaro, made the perfect entry point.

Patiently, Sophia waited behind two shepherds, who were exchanging angry words with each other. By their tones, she surmised they were handfasted.

"I told you, Gennaro, that damn dog was a waste of food. Lazy mutt."

"Imelda, I don't want to hear it. It was not his fault he lost a lamb to some wolf."

"Wolf? In these fields? Bah! I'll wager it was one of those fool Hunters."

Imelda's accusation piqued Sophia's interest... not to mention her desire to slit the woman's throat for insulting Sophia's people.

"You know, they only kill for the sake of killing. I think those three idiots on the Council should be sent out in the fields to rid us—"

Unaware the stranger behind them was tuning into what Imelda was saying, Gennaro *did* notice the guard was paying close attention to their conversation, perturbed when the latter's brow arched in anticipation of Imelda's next words.

Angling his body, until his back was to the guard, Gennaro faced his woman. "Now, Imelda, you know they are doing everything in their power to keep us safe." He inclined his head casually in the direction of the eavesdropping sentry. "Besides, I happened to see a pack of wolves migrating north a few days ago but thought it best not to worry you."

Imelda caught herself on the brink of an imprisonable offence for mocking their esteemed patriarchs. In a trice, she changed her tune and, hands on hips, chastised her mate. "Well, it would have been helpful if you had told me about the wolves in the first place."

The guard motioned to the woman. Abruptly, she stopped speaking.

Imelda, chewing on her bottom lip, handed over her documents.

You should be concerned, you foolish woman, Sophia chastised inwardly. *Never give them reason to commit your face and your name to memory.*

The guard took his time scrutinising the papers.

Snatching them back, Imelda came within a breath of the guard, alarm lacing her question, "Do you think, sir, he meant for me to be eaten by those wolves? I am afraid to go home with him... what if he stabs me in my sleep? Can I stay with—"

"Move along, woman," the guard instructed. "You are holding up traffic."

Sophia glanced over her shoulder but saw nobody behind her.

Huffing, Imelda countered, "If I am murdered tonight, I shall hold you personally responsible."

"Yeah, yeah," came the guard's bored response. He waved the pair through, the humour in Imelda's remark failing to register.

As Gennaro passed, the guard groused, "You would be doing the world a favour by volunteering to have your woman strung up with the other two."

Sophia's ears pricked up... *the other two?*

Gennaro pretended not to hear.

Imelda did, though, and when Gennaro caught up, administered a sharp tongue-lashing.

"Can you believe what that man said? And you... why did you do nothing to defend me?"

The bickering couple gone, it was Sophia's turn to step up to the guard.

"Pass," he said.

"Thank you." She deliberately misunderstood and set off through the gate.

Burly fingers clamped around her well-toned, slender arm, dragging her back. "And exactly where do you think you are going?"

Feigning innocence, Sophia replied, "Y-you told me to pass."

"Don't get smart with me. Show me your city permit."

"Why did you not say that in the first place?" Sophia castigated, rummaging around in the pockets of her frock.

Producing the grubby and mangled identity card, she handed it over, turning slightly in order to present more of her profile instead of facing him head on.

The guard was not the fool she had hoped he would be,

Swinging his gaze repeatedly between the picture and the woman in front of him, he struggled to see any resemblance. "Are you not supposed to look younger on your pass than in the flesh?"

He refrained from pointing out the cost of producing these passes. *Did she not realise the paraphernalia required was scarce?* Looking her up and down, he surmised she would not give two hoots.

"I guess I should take that as a compliment," Sophia quipped.

"And why is it I can hardly make out this name? Bia—"

"It is *Brigida*, you twit. If this is your job, you should learn to read."

"Watch your mouth. Why is it in such a mess?"

"You try spending your days tending to cattle and then tell me how clean the things you carry will remain."

There was a lengthy pause while the guard continued his scrutiny. Something was off but, in truth, he wasn't paid enough to be too meticulous, and this slip of a girl was no threat.

"If you're done, may I go?"

"Fine, be on your way." He returned her pass.

She risked one last question. "You mentioned something about a hanging today?"

"Yes, yes. The two who assassinated our beloved Signore

Regillus will pay for their crimes. Everyone in the city is to report to the old Stadio Olimpico by order of the surviving council members. Surely, you are aware of this?"

He's talking about Bianca and Gabriel. Merda. How in the hell am I going to prevent an execution? Covering her shock as well as her lack of knowledge with aplomb, Sophia nodded sagely, "Of course I am. I was simply confirming it was today. Time moves at a different pace in the fields, and I could easily be a day, or even two, early."

He accepted her argument, tenuous though it was. "You had best hurry. All residents must present their ticket and be seated by midday. You *do* have your ticket…?"

"No need to fret, sir. It is waiting for me on my kitchen table as we speak."

"I am glad to hear it. From what I understand, the penalty for missing the spectacle will be as severe as the execution.

"Then I shall hurry along. Thank you!"

<hr />

The closer Sophia got to her destination, the less confident she became. Her journey had taken her along the Via Flaminia Nuova and the Corsa di Francia, through districts normally swarming with people going about their day. All were unnervingly empty.

Worse, if her diminishing shadow was any indication, it was almost midday. With three kilometres to go, Sophia feared she would not reach the Stadio in time to save her kin.

The warning from the sentry at the gate increased her distress.

What will happen to the others if I am caught and killed? Sophia agonised. *The idea of the brothers attempting to reign over the caravans is more frightening than any possible punish…*

The memory of Angelo maintaining a solitary vigil on the

riverbank, and the two soldiers she saw in the shattered husk of the village, feet from where she ordered Angelo to land, tugged at her heart.

She quickened her pace.

"I cannot wallow in self-doubt and allow him to be sacrificed because I faltered," she swore to herself.

Taking a right onto the Via del Foro Italico, Sophia began to sprint. Her effort might prove futile, but she had to try.

Her dress whipped back and forth, hampering her speed.

A voice in her head taunted, "Pitiful wench. Stop putting on such a brave face. Your sister would be served better if you curled up in some back alley and died."

Another chimed in, "True, anyone can see how tired you are... even that old horse clomping up behind you. Why do you not let it trample you—"

"*Fermare*," Sophia yelled.

The drowsy old man in semi-control of the wagon, allowing the horse to lead him to their destination, rather than the other way around, lurched awake at the sound of the woman's bawled command.

Yanking the ageing leather reins, he pulled the wandering horse to a halt within centimetres of Sophia.

Sophia stared at the mare for a moment, daring to stroke its nose. The creature tossed her head at the loving touch, nickering softly.

The man called down to her, "Signorina, step aside and allow us to pass. We are running late, and I do not need this nag thinking you are about to give her a treat."

Her fingers intertwined in the chestnut mare's bridle, Sophia inquired, "*Buonuomo*, please excuse me, but might I ask where you and this handsome beast are heading?"

The man cocked his head, partially at the absurdity of the question... but mostly because no one had ever referred to him as, *good man.*

"To the Stadio, where else? After those two have finished their dance at the end of the hangman's rope, Belle and I are tasked with removing the corpses." He spotted the woman's fingers tightening on the harness as he spoke. Unbidden, he recalled the disturbing stories about the night the Hunters had stormed the city, and how the guards swore they would return.

Still, this stranger did not look like a crazed killer, as opposed to the two awaiting him... at least that was the impression he had gained from the rumours flying about.

His voice held a hint of agitation. "I cannot tarry, the Council will be unhappy if I fail to show up by noon."

Coming to his side of the wagon, Sophia entreated. "Sir, I beg you, please allow me to ride along with you. I will never arrive in time and am afraid of the consequences if I am caught missing the execution of the murderers."

The old man stroked his straggly grey beard, sizing her up. *I am sure I can take her if she tries anything. In fact, I kinda hope she does.* He hid a smirk, a plan to exact payment for his generosity already percolating. *This donna will be unable to refuse my gracious invitation to join me unless she wishes to find herself answering to the authorities.*

He shuffled and let his legs splay out. "*Sì, femmina.* I will be more than happy to play your knight. Unfortunately, you will have to ride in the back. The seat is not quite large enough for two."

If she *did* guess what he had in store for her, he reckoned in the time it took for her to jump off the wagon, he could catch hold of her hair, or that stupid frock.

Looking between the man and the filthy bed of the wagon, Sophia arched an incredulous brow. Inwardly acknowledging his desperation to get to the Stadio probably outweighed his baser proclivities, she huffed a resigned sigh and, using the wheel to help, hoisted herself over the wooden side of the cart.

Beggars cannot be picky... or something like that.

19

S ophia felt the wagon jerk as the old man, whom she secretly nicknamed Greybeard, clicked his tongue, encouraging the horse to continue towards the Stadio. Scanning the bed of the cart for the least soiled place to sit, she noticed a folded tarp in one corner.

No doubt to cover the bodies.

Conceding it was preferable to the layers of muck, Sophia sank onto it, made herself as comfortable as possible and, in an effort to be courteous, introduced herself, "I am Brigida."

"Good for you."

There was a lull in conversation for the next fifteen minutes as the wagon trundled along.

Sophia was a product of architecture. During various sorties into Rome, if she happened across a book on the subject, she would make sure to 'borrow' it.

Without fail, her comrades disapproved. Given their limited carrying capacity, they had better things to seize than items considered frivolities. The Padrona's daughter, Sophia got away with what the others would not risk.

She had amassed an encyclopaedic knowledge of the city and was puzzled by the choice of venue for the executions.

To fill in time, she quizzed, "Why, with all the impressive monuments in the city, did the Council decide on such a squalid place when the Colosseum is much easier to get to and offers a far more dramatic backdrop? Are they not concerned the stands will collapse under the weight of so many spectators? Or that they will probably fall ill from all the rust."

Greybeard looked over his shoulder. "Not my problem. And has anybody said you talk too much? In my family, women are seen and not heard. It is a lesson you would be wise to learn."

Nettled by his medieval attitude, Sophia was about to give him a piece of her mind when a raucous din reached their ears, and the rebuke died in her throat.

The Stadio Olimpico loomed up ahead of them.

"*Merda,*" the old man grumbled, snapping the reins against the horse. "Move along, Belle, they have already started."

The mare did her best to race along the last five hundred metres like a thoroughbred in her prime, her ageing heart pounding with each clomp of a hoof on the hard pavement, breath bursting from her nose in pained snorts.

Nearing the service entrance to the Stadio, Greybeard warned Sophia, "Girl, you'd be smart to hide under that tarp."

Sophia did not bother to ask why. Questioning his reasons took time she didn't have, and she was ready should they prove nefarious.

Unfurling the tarp, she slid beneath it. Unable to see,

Sophia concentrated on listening intently for any pending danger.

It did not take long for it to find her.

The horse and wagon came to a stop. Over Belle's panting, Sophia discerned the approach of boots.

A churlish voice spoke, "You call this being on time? A dead man could have arrived faster, you dolt. You have no idea what it took to convince the Council to hire you for this job, and how do you thank me? You make me look a fool in front of the entire city... never mind the triumvirate.

"Bad enough your tardiness forced them to stall the proceedings until your lazy ass showed up, the new head councillor used the delay to demonstrate his complete lack of prowess in the art of public-speaking. A stuck pig is more eloquent."

As if to underscore the speaker's point, an obsequious whine reached them through the long tunnel.

"Don't tell me they promoted bloody Faraldo?"

Sophia detected shock, dismay, and disillusionment in Greybeard's question, and smothered an irreverent urge to giggle.

"Okay, I won't tell you, that way you will be surprised." The voice sniped.

She heard the old man huff, "That's it, Rome is doomed."

An awkward pause hung in the air, stretching out until even Sophia felt uncomfortable.

About to throw off the tarp and kill them both, her hand was stayed when the old man griped, "Are you done, or shall I be even later because of you?"

"Get onto the field, and do not forget my cut."

"Yeah, yeah," the reply, a resentful grunt.

Sophia heard the snap of reins and the click of a tongue, then felt the cart roll.

They had not made it two metres before 'Boots' barked, "Hold on. What the hell do you have in the back of the wagon?"

The wheels ground to a halt.

Sophia withdrew her blade.

"Are you trying to get *me* executed as well?" Boots demanded. "Please don't tell me you are smuggling somebody in."

Sophia readied herself should the guard decide to lift the tarp.

Instead, she heard the old man lie without missing a beat, "Oh, that? Found a corpse on the way over. I'm guessing your subordinates overlooked this one. She's been in the sun for a couple of days, so is nothing to look at, but if you have a strong stomach—"

Tacitly, Sophia agreed — the muck in the wagon *did* reek of death.

In response to the oblique challenge, Boots changed his tune. "Do not think the city will pay you for *that* disposal. You have no way of proving cause of death."

"Hmm... so her missing head is not proof enough those barbarians took the girl's life? I will make sure to dump the body on your front step."

A crack of leather and the wagon lurched forwards.

The echo of hooves clomping on concrete informed Sophia, she and the old man had entered the service tunnel leading to the field.

She had mere seconds to spring the plan she had been concocting from the moment she climbed into the wagon.

Peeking out from under the tarp, she surmised by the lack of light they had reached the middle of the passageway.

She smiled grimly and tossed off the canvas. Before the old man could ask what the hell she was doing, he felt her surprisingly strong arm wrap around his throat, cutting off his supply of oxygen and reducing his pleas to garbled bleats.

He scrabbled to dislodge her, in the same instant as he experienced an excruciating pain in his side.

Sophia stabbed her razor-sharp blade into the old man's rib cage, puncturing his right lung between his second and third rib. As she twisted the blade deeper, the tip lacerated his heart.

Tightening her stranglehold, she skewered the knife back and forth, maximising the damage, until he stopped struggling.

He went limp in her grasp. Sophia released him, her lip curling sardonically as his body rolled off the wagon.

Jumping down, she retrieved his dirty coat and hat. Suppressing a shudder, her nose crinkling in distaste, she shrugged them on.

The roar of the crowd grew louder, triggering a sorrowful thought. *If I am too late, at least I shall be able to recover their bodies and send them off with the honour they deserve.*

Clambering onto the wagon's bench, Sophia gathered the reins and, in gentle tones, coaxed the horse to move — to no avail.

Unaccustomed to being addressed kindly, the request confused Belle and she hesitated, a decision which produced a solid whack on her rump.

Disinclined to suffer an encore, the mare resumed her slow plod along the tunnel.

Horse and wagon emerged onto a field once reserved for men to chase a ball up and down perfectly manicured grass for hours.

Sophia brought Belle to a standstill and surveyed her surroundings. Her stomach roiled.

In the middle of the brown, weed infected turf, a makeshift scaffold had been erected. On top, stood two figures.

While horrific, the sight gave Sophia a modicum of solace.

*I am **not** too late.*

20

Bianca and Gabriel looked worse for wear. Bruised faces, testament to beatings which could not have occurred during the bid to rescue Aurora; bedraggled clothing no doubt concealing equally battered bodies.

Sophia directed the horse to the crude structure.

She listened with half an ear as a man, presumably the aforementioned Faraldo, with a megaphone bawled at the crowds in the rickety grandstands. His rhetoric, little more than propaganda to bolster support for the elite.

His speech impediment, while detracting somewhat from his delivery, did not blunt his message.

"...and let this b-be a w-warning to any w-who doubt our resolve and strength. You too w-will find yourselves dangling at the end of a rope."

The stands erupted in wild applause. A few brave souls risked stomping their feet on the chipped and splintered boards.

Belle gave a disapproving snort, for all the world as though deploring the choice of leader. Signore Faraldo's attention swivelled to the wagon rumbling into the centre of the arena.

He jabbed a furious finger at the pair, then paused. Although irritating, their late arrival *did* present him with a prime example, on which he could capitalise — in front of the entire populace no less. *Am I about to look a gift horse in the mouth… literally…? I most certainly am not.* He chuckled inwardly at his fine wit.

"As y-you can see, cit-citi- people of Rome, it is impossible to get dependable help from you. You plead for your superiors to defend you in the bad times, b-but refuse to return the favour when the situation is reversed.

"Consider yourselves lucky we of the Council…"

He gestured to his colleagues with a grand flourish, which included the newest member standing alongside. The recent recruit, a certain Signore Callixtus from a venerable family, had the demeanour of a man coerced into service under sufferance and who, it was glaringly obvious, wanted no part of the proceedings.

The spectators watched the pompous, self-appointed figurehead drone on.

"…are on constant watch to prevent the likes of these two bar-bar… wicked killers from slaking their appetite for butchery in their quest to destroy our glorious city."

An accusation which barely raised the obligatory cheer from the assemblage.

Sophia pulled the old man's hat further down over her eyes, apparently trying to hide herself from the embarrassment of delaying the *entertainment.*

Outraged, Signore Faraldo marched over to berate the hired hand. "D-Do not expect f-full p-payment," he railed. "By rights, you ought to be tossed into some d-dank cell and forgotten."

Her head bowed, Sophia lifted a gloved hand in weary acknowledgment of his chastisement.

Torn between preserving his dignity and disciplining the driver for his appalling lack of respect, the man opted for the former and turned away.

This was Sophia's moment. With the speed and agility of a cat, she leapt down from her seat, to catch him from behind.

The two tumbled across the field.

Murmurs drifted from the grandstands as the attendees strained to figure out what was happening.

Forcing the councillor to his knees, Sophia held her knife, caked with the blood of the old man, against his throat, nicking the soft, flabby skin.

She bellowed, "Enough of this lunacy. Release them, now..." vowing retribution if they failed to comply, "or I will carve up the lot of you."

Transfixed, those in front of the gallows gawked at Sophia, causing her to increase her pressure on the blade. "You want to see a sample of my work? Hangman, free them. Do *not* make me repeat myself."

The executioner glanced at the two remaining Council members. Tight lipped, the elder did not respond, but Signore Callixtus nodded his consent. It was enough to send the hangman up the steps.

The idea he might get away with kicking the stands from under the accused died before it fully formed, the merciless glower of the woman leaving him in no doubt of the repercussions. Carefully, but with haste, he removed the nooses and helped the pair down from the boxes.

Bianca shrugged off the man's hand and ran to Gabriel. Uncaring that they had an audience, the couple embraced, then shared the kind of heartfelt kiss reserved for partners whose love transcended their lives.

Sophia rolled her eyes. "Hey, lovebirds, plenty of time for

that later. Get down here before these *compassionate* men change their minds."

Her blade biting into Signore Faraldo's throat, Sophia transferred her wrath to the crowd.

"You, cowardly dogs. You call yourselves civilised, yet you clamour for the death of my sister and her mate in an unbridled frenzy."

Gabriel and Bianca, who were climbing into the rear of the wagon, paused at Sophia's words.

Sophia had barely begun.

"You hypocrites make me sick. It is true, my people suffer from a congenital condition which robs us of empathy — that elusive emotion you believe you possess. We never asked for this, it was a curse wrought by some unseen hand.

"Instead of using your gift to help and understand, you shunned us. You made us scapegoats for your perceived misfortunes and treated us as lesser mortals who should be grateful you permit our existence at all.

"You drove us from your cities, designating us as dangerous. Well, to use a term you feeble-minded farmers can understand, you reap what you sow.

"You have deluded yourselves into thinking, because your homes are not on wheels and you cower behind your walls, you are somehow superior."

Sophia's voice quivered with anger and repudiation.

She steadied herself.

"Yet… yet the moment a miracle occurred in *our* camp, your true colours surfaced… and black does not become you. So brainwashed are you by these power-hungry maniacs…"

Sophia yanked Signore Faraldo's head back by the hair to expose his face, emphasising her point.

"…that you were prepared to let them sacrifice an innocent babe. Sheep have more autonomy. Then, when the child's parents fought to save her... as any self-respecting kin would... you bayed for their deaths.

"Your arrogance knows no bounds and your pitiless savagery far exceeds ours. We do not kill for fun, or to examine the entrails of an infant in the hopes of unlocking the secret of life. We kill because you left us no choice. We mount the heads of our victims as a reminder not to fall into the same soulless trap."

The silence in the arena was complete. Sophia's censure reached every single citizen.

Without relinquishing her grip on the gibbering autocrat at her feet, she swung the knife in a broad arc.

"From this day on, I pledge our people will not set foot in this city of the damned. We do not need to be contaminated by your ilk. But mark my words, if any of you wander on our lands to the north uninvited, the reprisals will be swift and dire. They will make our last incursion into Rome seem like a picnic in the Piazza Navona."

No one moved, the whole stadium was paralysed by shame.

Satisfied she had got her message across, Sophia bent to whisper in her captive's ear. "Remember this day. The day you were spared when, by rights, you ought to be tossed in a dank dungeon and forgotten."

Not waiting for his response, she rammed him face first into the dirt, sprang up onto the driver's seat of the cart and grabbed the reins, wheeling Belle around.

As the horse bolted for the tunnel, Signore Faraldo hauled himself upright. Brushing the dust off his clothes, he exhorted the guards, "Apprehend the outlaws before they escape."

His orders went unheeded.

Without a backwards glance, Sophia snapped the reins.

Horse and wagon hurtled into the gloom, racing for freedom.

The silhouette of a man appeared in the archway, demanding they halt.

Sophia knew that voice.

Boots.

There was a short-lived stand-off during which Sophia made no effort to slow Belle, and Boots refused to move. She allowed herself a split-second's admiration of his fortitude, then he vanished under the mare's thundering hooves, and the wagon with its precious cargo emerged from the tunnel.

From there, they fled from the depths of the malodorous city to the fresh air of the north.

Belle trotted into the dead township as the setting sun kissed the horizon. The darkening sky cast an ominous pall over the empty streets. Long shadows like grasping fingers crept from the corners of every building as though on the prowl for unsuspecting prey.

A chill autumnal wind moaned, adding to the unearthly atmosphere, unsettling Sophia, who was already tense.

Struggling to comprehend they were safe, and not victims of some hunger-induced dream, Gabriel and Bianca shivered and huddled together for warmth. Their threadbare garments offered meagre protection. Gabriel gathered Bianca against his chest, fearing her reserves, depleted after their stint in prison, would not be enough to ward off the breeze.

Relishing the heat from her mate's body, Bianca nestled in his arms.

Soon they would be home and reunited with their daughter.

While the wagon rumbled through the dilapidated hamlet, Sophia kept her eyes peeled for any hint of movement which might indicate Angelo's hiding place.

Dread clawed at her as they approached the end of Settebagni without any luck. Uncaring that she might alert a lurking city guard or ten, Sophia shouted to the twilight, "Angelo, show your stupid self or I will leave your miserable hide here."

Gabriel and Bianca stared at each other, then up at Sophia in disbelief, detecting the concern in her voice.

A figure materialised from behind a withered tree. Clutching his side, he limped onto the road.

In the last gasp of daylight, Sophia recognised Angelo. In addition to his hunched posture, which spoke volumes, she spied patches of discolouration on his face and clothing. *Blood... and, if so, was it his or someone else's?*

Before anyone could blink, she was off the seat and running to meet him. Supporting him on the side he wasn't favouring, she helped him to the wagon.

"What the hell happened to you? Did you get drunk and fall down the embankment?" she screeched.

"I-it's nothing," he defended. "T-the patrol stumbled across the boat and decided to claim ownership of it. Naturally, we disagreed. One of the cowards grabbed an oar and attacked me from behind."

Sophia's accusatory tone morphed into one of compassion. "D-did he break your ribs? Puncture a lung? Are you dying?"

Angelo stopped in his tracks to study her curiously. "And what would you do if I said yes?"

To her chagrin, Sophia blushed, relieved the dusk masked her heightened colour. With studied deliberation, she lowered her shoulder, letting Angelo slither to the ground... ensuring he did not land on his injured ribs.

Resuming her seat on the wagon, she reverted to her usual insouciance. "Don't bother dragging your ass back to camp. No sense wasting good wine on your funeral. Wait..." a thought struck her. "...where *is* the boat?"

Angelo scratched his chin, pondering his reply carefully. "If you take into consideration the weight of the boat minus any possible damage it might have sustained in the fray, and the speed of the current—"

Sophia interrupted his rambling. "It's at the bottom of the Tiber, isn't it?"

"That would be my guess."

Shaking her head in irritation, she grumbled over her shoulder to Gabriel. "If you can see fit to stop groping my sister for a moment, will you load this idiot in the back with you. Please hurry. It is late and I'm hungry!"

EPILOGUE

Autumn mists surrendered to winter snows, which in turn yielded to the vibrant blossoms of spring.

True to Sophia's promise, the Hunters did not return to Rome. Any sorties focused on the tribes further north.

When the warmer weather returned, Gabriel endeavoured to convince the camp to try their hand at planting. His requests were met with emphatic rejections. Did he not realise such a menial chore was beneath them?

Inevitably, the discussion deteriorated into fistfights, the Hunters taken by surprise when, in most cases, Gabriel came out on top. That his success could be credited to Bianca's training, was something the couple in question never revealed.

In return for sharing his knowledge, Gabriel pestered the enterprising Hunters to explain how they operated their powerful lights and the smelly thing they called a generator. While he was quite happy with the status quo, a voice at the back of his mind insisted this information might be important.

Ensconced in Noemi's caravan, an occasional squeal prompted Bianca to glance up from her reading. A doting smile lit her face as she watched Aurora scoot across the floor in pursuit of her latest toy.

When not tending to her daughter, Bianca had devoted the months since her return to the encampment reviewing Noemi's notes on procedures and medicine. Not only those related to pregnancy and birth, but also the numerous other illnesses Noemi had come across in her travels.

Interestingly, she had figured out how Aurora and she had survived the birth. Turned out it was simply the law of natural selection. The most resilient of any species tended to be those who bred outside their societal pool. Gabriel and she came from opposite groups, their differences proved to be the catalyst.

This had given rise to plenty of discussion among the women, especially those in a relationship where either themselves or their mate were of mixed heritage. The odds no longer stacked against them, a handful were currently in the early stages of pregnancy.

Anxiety about the actual birth had not wholly diminished, but the pervading opinion was that this new-found knowledge gave mother and child a fighting chance and the risk was worth it.

Rumours of Bianca's burgeoning medical skills had reached the new government in Rome, who had yet to fill the late Dr Vincenzo's position.

When details emerged that culpability for the *Notte di Morte* — as it became known — lay solely at the feet of the original Council, the citizens arose, *en masse*, to exile the two older members.

Rome appointed Signore Callixtus, the reluctant recruit

and a man purported to be incorruptible, to reorganise the city. His first order of business was to establish a stable peace with the Hunters, which included lengthy discussions with the camp's Padrona.

Eventually, those inside the walls ventured north to seek medical help... and training.

Bianca looked up to see Sophia enter the caravan carrying two cups of the brew Noemi had called coffee.

Accepting one, she took a gulp, then observed, "If you inhale deeply, you can still catch a hint of mother's cigarettes. It's almost like she is still here."

Her brow furrowed, Sophia sat down and huffed, "If she was, she would beat your ass for your decision."

"I do not understand why you are so upset, Soph. It's not as though I am leaving you... not entirely."

"You might as well be. It is supposed to be *you* not me leading the tribe. I know how to fight, but not how to govern."

"Seriously? You more than demonstrated your proficiency when you rescued Gabriel and me."

"Bah, the only reason *I* did that was because if I had left it to Angelo or Antonio, they would have ended up on the gibbet with you."

"Speaking of the brothers, which—"

"Do not finish that question!"

Bianca laughed at the disdain on Sophia's face, which elicited a kick on the shin.

"Besides..." Sophia added under her breath. "According to you, there are more men around here than those in the camp." She sipped her coffee, her expression inscrutable.

Bianca lifted a puzzled brow at the offhand comment, and she leant on her elbows, expectantly.

Her sister refused to elaborate. Giving up... for now... Bianca settled back in her seat and returned to the original topic of discussion.

"Okay, okay. I will behave. And, as I was saying, we are not vanishing into the wilds. We're a short boat ride or a slightly longer horse ride away. It's easier for the Romans to find us there, than constantly traipsing through the camp, disturbing everyone."

Sophia brooded, "But you will not be here to lead."

"No, but you are perfectly capable of assuming the role, Soph. Trust me, I would not be leaving if I didn't believe in you. Plus, you have Nicoletta. *No one* is more suited to serve as your security, Padrona."

"Until that child in her belly decides to show himself... then who the hell knows?"

"When he does, make sure to send for me."

Bianca heard her name being hailed. It was time.

Swallowing the last of her coffee, she closed the book and slipped it into the bag hanging off the back of the chair. Rising from her seat, Bianca scooped up her giggling daughter, and slung the bag over her shoulder. With one last look around the caravan, she followed Sophia out into the sunshine.

On the driver's seat of a smart new wagon, Gabriel waited.

Today marked the start of a new adventure.

Sophia hugged her sister and niece, grumbling, "Bianca, you know I hate you."

"Take care of everyone, Sophia. And I love you, too."

Bianca handed Aurora to Gabriel, and clambered up to settle next to him. She waved to the assembled Hunters reassuring them, they would always be within reach.

With a whistle and a flick of the reins, Belle ambled forwards. The journey south to their new home had begun.

The wagon had been rattling along the badly maintained road for several minutes when Gabriel remarked, "I have to confess, I am surprised Sophia allowed you to leave."

Bianca nodded, "Aye. Almost as surprised as the day we divulged our plans, and she did not take your head."

There was more truth than humour in Bianca's statement. Gabriel did not respond but the horse picked up her pace. The quicker they put a distance between the camp's new Padrona and himself, the easier he would breathe.

While their destination was not far, a few hours at the most, in truth, it might as well be to the moon and beyond.

From this point on, their lives would never be the same.

None of that mattered.

The past was done, its echoes fading like the paintings they saw in the Castel.

Yes, they would face hardships and obstacles, who didn't? Life was not some superficial illusion, it was harsh, painful, and gritty, and often tripped up the unwary. It was also extraordinarily beautiful, and to experience all its facets was a blessing not to be abused or taken for granted.

Their new abode in sight, the quietly soporific rumble of the cart was interrupted by a distant roar. Akin to thunder, there was an unidentifiable, and definitely unnatural, resonance to the sound which seemed to be rolling down from the north.

Concerned, Bianca asked, "Is that a storm?"

"Nothing to worry about, love." Gabriel reassured. "Too far away. It'll have blown out long before it reaches us."

"Good, I hate storms."

Gabriel chuckled and patted her knee. "I know, love, I know. Look, our new home." As expected, his remark diverted Bianca whose face lit up in eager anticipation, pointing out the features to Aurora, who had no idea what her mama was talking about, but babbled in childish excitement anyway.

As they trundled up the gravelled driveway, Bianca caught Gabriel's eyes over Aurora's head. The smile the couple shared, more eloquent than any words. The future was uncertain, and the road might be rocky but, together, they would prevail.

Their bond, forged in a snowy field and strengthened in a city under siege, became indissoluble when, without hesitation, each was willing to sacrifice themselves for the other in the name of love.

ABOUT THE AUTHOR
RORI BLEU

With a smattering of riverboat pirates and royalty in her heritage, Rori Bleu's childhood reflected her past.
An interest in fairy tales, myth and legend were as important as spirited discussions around politics and current affairs — although some might argue they are one and the same!

A fascination, sparked by listening to Grimm's Fairy Tales at her grandmother's knee, not only encouraged Rori's passion for reading, but also steered her into the world of RPG's. What began as a fun pastime, soon evolved into the creation of fantastical worlds, but Rori never lost her love of politics going on to specialise in Governmental History and Historical Research.

ABOUT THE AUTHOR
ROSIE CHAPEL

Rosie Chapel lives in Perth, Australia with her hubby and three furkids. When not writing, she loves catching up with friends, burying herself in a book (or three), discovering the wonders of Western Australia, or — and the best — a quiet evening at home with her husband, enjoying a glass of wine and a movie.

Website: www.rosiechapel.com

ALSO BY RORI BLEU

Pineapple Meringue

Imprisoned Hearts

Port of London

Dani's Masquerade

Black Tulips

Ajei's Destiny

Porta Aeternum

ALSO BY ROSIE CHAPEL

Links to Rosie's books can be found at
www.rosiechapel.com

His Fiery Hoyden

A Regency Duet

A Regency Christmas Double

Fate is Curious

A Christmas Prayer *with Ashlee Shades*

The Lady's Wager

Winning Emma

A Love Impossible

Unravelling Roana

Love Kindled

<u>Fairy Tale Romance</u>

Chasing Bluebells

<u>Contemporary Romances</u>

Of Ruins and Romance

All At Once It's You

Cobweb Dreams

Just One Step

His Heart's Second Sigh

www.ingramcontent.com/pod-product-compliance
Lightning Source LLC
Chambersburg PA
CBHW072145130726
47909CB00004BB/1186